PLEASE

P L E

PETER DARBYSHIRE
A S E

a NOVEL

RAINCOAST BOOKS
Vancouver

Copyright © 2002 by Peter Darbyshire.

All rights reserved. Raincoast Books is a member of CANCOPY (Canadian Copyright Licensing Agency). No part of this publication may be reproduced, stored in a retrieval system or transmitted in any form or by any means without prior written permission from the publisher, or, in case of photocopying or other reprographic copying, a licence from CANCOPY, One Yonge Street, Toronto, Ontario, M5E 1E5.

Raincoast Books acknowledges the ongoing financial support of the Government of Canada through The Canada Council for the Arts and the Book Publishing Industry Development Program (BPIDP); and the Government of British Columbia through the BC Arts Council.

Edited by Lynn Henry
Text design by Ingrid Paulson
Typeset by Teresa Bubela

NATIONAL LIBRARY OF CANADA CATALOGUING IN PUBLICATION DATA

Darbyshire, Peter, 1967–
  Please

ISBN 1-55192-562-1

  I. Title.
PS8557.A59346P6 2002   C813'.6   C2002-910550-1
PR9199.4.D37P6 2002

LIBRARY OF CONGRESS CONTROL NUMBER: 2002091840

Raincoast Books   *In the United States:*
9050 Shaughnessy Street   Publishers Group West
Vancouver, British Columbia   1700 Fourth Street
Canada   V6P 6E5   Berkeley, California
www.raincoast.com   94710

At Raincoast Books we are committed to protecting the environment and to the responsible use of natural resources. We are acting on this commitment by working with suppliers and printers to phase out our use of paper produced from ancient forests. This book is one step towards that goal. We are working with Markets Initiative (www.oldgrowthfree.com) on this project.

Printed in Canada by Friesens.

10 9 8 7 6 5 4 3 2 1

7 | I Couldn't Live Like That

18 | Could I Afford You?

30 | This Isn't What I Wanted

41 | Please

53 | What Happened to Our Baby?

71 | Jesus Cured My Herpes

84 | Where We Live

92 | It's Not My Responsibility

102 | Happily Ever After, I Guess

122 | Are You Sure You Don't Want to Kill Him?

133 | He'll Live Forever

142 | Hell Believes in You

157 | How Long Does This Sort of Thing Usually Take?

166 | Still

171 | It Doesn't Get Any Better

182 | There's Nothing Wrong With Me

I COULDN'T LIVE LIKE THAT

I WALKED EVERYWHERE in those days. I had a car but I couldn't always afford gas. Sometimes, at night, I went up to the windows of houses and looked inside. In the dark, you can stand right on the other side of the glass, and no one ever knows you're there. From the street, these places always seem like the kind of homes you see in magazine ads, all red walls and leather furniture. Close up, though, it's mostly just people watching television or doing the dishes. Although once I saw a woman feeding soup to a man with two broken legs. There was nothing wrong with his arms but she fed him soup anyway, kneeling beside him on the couch and carefully lifting the spoon to his lips.

Another time I saw a man putting on eyeliner. I was standing deep in a driveway between houses and looking into a bedroom. I could see him through the cracks between the blinds. He was sitting at a vanity with lights around the mirror. When he was done with the eyeliner he put on eye shadow and lipstick. Then he cleaned his face with a tissue and blew himself a kiss. After that, he walked out of the room and didn't come back. I wondered whose makeup it was. His wife's? His roommate's?

And once I came across another man doing the same thing as me. I started down a driveway and saw him kneeling on the ground at the other end, his face shining from the light of the basement window in front of him. He never looked away from it, not even when I went back up the driveway. I don't think he ever knew I was there. I never went back to that house again.

I was twenty-three or twenty-four at the time, I can't really remember anymore. I hadn't worked in months. My wife had left me. Sometimes I woke up with shooting pains in my stomach, like someone had stabbed me while I slept. The doctors said there was nothing wrong with me.

ON ONE OF THESE walks I met a blind man. It was around five or six in the evening. I could tell he was blind by the fact that he wore those dark glasses and he was tapping around the base of a telephone pole with a long, white cane. When I tried to walk around him, he swung the cane into my legs. It bent like it was made of rubber. I had to stop because he kept the cane in front of me. I couldn't move without jumping over it.

"I'm a little lost," he said, as if I'd asked him how he was. "There's not a newspaper box around here, is there?"

"No, there's nothing but the telephone pole," I told him.

"There's supposed to be a newspaper box," he said, "but I guess my counting got thrown off somewhere."

"Yes, that's most likely it," I agreed, even though I didn't really know what he was talking about. I waited for him to move the cane but he didn't.

"I was walking to the school," he went on. "But I should have come across it by now. You don't see a school anywhere, do you?"

I looked around. We were standing in front of an old Victorian house with vines growing up the front of it. A young girl in white pajamas stood in the front window, watching us. There weren't any lights on behind her. She was just a white silhouette against the darkness. I wondered where her parents were.

"No," I said, "there's nothing but houses around here."

"Wow," he said, shaking his head. "I'm really messed up."

The girl didn't move at all, didn't even seem to blink. She looked like a ghost, and for some reason, that thought reminded me of the last night I ever saw my wife.

"I could really use some help here," the blind man said.

THE BLIND MAN KEPT his free hand on my arm while we walked, as if he was afraid I would run away if he didn't. All the way down the street, he tapped the ground in front of us with his cane and counted under his breath. Now that I was taking him back the way he had come, he seemed to know exactly where we were at all times. Every intersection we took, he guided me in a different direction. Soon I was the one who was lost.

"I have it all memorized," he told me as we went along. "I go for the same walk, to the school and back, every night. Turn left out the door, two hundred and twenty steps to the first right, four hundred and ten from there..." He went on like that for some time and then ended with, "And that box has always been there before, a hundred steps from the intersection, give or take, after the second left turn. Always. I don't understand it."

"How do you know when you're actually at the school?" I wanted to know. "I mean, even if you take the proper amount of steps, how do you know it's the school and not something else, like a bank or a high-rise?" I pictured him tapping his way around a building, trying to figure out what it was just by its size and shape. Maybe counting taps like he did steps.

"I can hear the kids," he told me. "There are always kids in the playground, even in the middle of the night. It's like they don't know where else to go."

Later, he said, "You're probably wondering why I go to the school every day."

"No, not really."

"I'm not after any Lolitas, if you know what I mean."

"No, I don't."

HE LED ME TO a large house with a fence around the front yard. The fence was taller than me and had trees all around the inside of it. The address was printed on the door, in red paint. It looked like a child had done it.

"Here we are," he said.

"Why do you have such a big fence?" I asked. None of the other houses on the street had fences around their front yards.

"It's so no one can see us," he said. "I think the neighbours complained or something."

"Us?" I asked.

"It's kind of like a group home," he said. "For people like me."

I pictured a whole houseful of blind men, bumping around the halls and asking each other for help just to get out the door.

"Would you like to come in?" he asked. "For a coffee or something?"

"I don't think so," I said.

"Maybe something to eat," he said. "I can make you a sandwich."

"No, I've really got places to be," I told him.

"I have drugs."

HE LED ME THROUGH the front door, which wasn't locked. As soon as he opened the door I heard a woman scream, then the sounds of gunshots. I was ready to run away, or maybe hide behind one of the trees, but he walked in like this was normal, so I followed him.

Just inside the entranceway was a large living room, and this was where all the noise was coming from. Two men were sitting on a couch underneath the window, watching a big-screen Sony across the room. On the television, some cops in black body armor were standing around a man lying on the ground. He was wearing nothing but shorts, and blood was running out of several bullet holes in his upper body. A woman was standing on the porch of a house in the background, and she was the one who was screaming. I wasn't entirely sure, but I thought I might have seen this before.

The two men on the couch turned to look at us when we came in, but they didn't say anything. One of them raised a beer can to his lips. "Hello," I said. They still didn't say anything.

"Don't mind them," the blind man said. "They're deaf."

They looked back at the television when the scene changed to an outdoors shot. Now a bear was mauling someone on the other side of a parked car. Someone had videotaped the whole thing rather than help. The deaf men started laughing, making noises like barking dogs.

"It's just down this way," the blind man said, leading me deeper into the house.

FOR A WHILE during these days I dated a woman who had a metal arm. It was the first woman I'd been with since my wife. She'd lost her real arm in a car accident. She talked about the accident like it didn't mean anything to her. "We were going too fast around a corner and the car rolled. That was it, just one of those stupid, one-car accidents." She never said who the other person was, or which one of them was driving. "Silly me, I had my arm hanging out the window and it got torn off when the car rolled over it." *Silly me.* She really said that.

She didn't mind having a metal arm at all. Not that it looked metal. When you put it beside her real arm, you could barely tell them apart. But when you touched this fake arm, it was cold and hard.

And it would move on its own. She would take it off and lay it on her dresser, but the fingers would twitch for hours afterwards, and sometimes the elbow would even bend. "It's just going to sleep," she told me. But one night she was moving around and whimpering with some dream, and the arm matched all her movements. It jerked and shook on the dresser, and the fingers balled up into a fist, and then the whole thing fell on the floor. I wouldn't get out of bed the next morning until she'd picked it up and put it back on.

She lived in a basement apartment with only one window. We had to leave the bedroom door open while we slept for fear we'd suffocate. She couldn't afford anything else because all she had was some sort of disability pension. She wanted to be an actress but she hadn't worked as anything but an extra in years. Who would hire a woman with only one arm?

We liked to tour condos that were for sale. Only the new ones, though, never anything that had already been lived in. We'd walk through them and make notes in a little notebook we'd bought, talk about the view, look in the cupboards. The salespeople acted like they believed we could actually afford these places.

One woman opened a bottle of wine for us while we were there. She gave it to us in little plastic glasses. "I'm sorry about that," she said, "but would you believe someone actually stole our real wineglasses?" It was the best wine I'd ever had.

When the woman asked us what we did, I told her I was a marketer for IBM, and my girlfriend said she was a nurse.

This woman showed us around the model suite. When she brought us to the living room, the sun was just setting, as if she'd cued it. The entire place filled with a golden light, and I held my girlfriend's hand — the real one — until it passed.

"Now there's a Kodak moment if I've ever seen one," the saleswoman said.

My girlfriend stood in the middle of the smaller bedroom and looked around. It was a young boy's room, with blue walls and a bed in the shape of a race car. "We'd want to paint, of course," she said. "When we have the children."

"Are you expecting?" the saleswoman asked.

"Oh no," my girlfriend said. "But someday." She looked at me and laughed.

"Cheers then," the saleswoman said and refilled our glasses.

She took us into the kitchen last and sat us down around a glass-topped table. There was an espresso maker on the counter and the fridge had an icemaker.

"Does the place come with all the appliances?" I asked.

"Oh yes," the woman said. "And there's a pool and a sauna in the building."

"A pool and a sauna," I repeated.

"That's right."

"And we don't have to pay for that?" my girlfriend asked. "We can just use it like everyone else?"

The woman gave us a blank contract to look at, and a pamphlet full of measurements and costs. I looked at all the numbers and said, "I don't know. I think it's a bit more than we wanted to pay."

"It always is," she said, still smiling.

"I mean, I don't know if we can afford a place like this," I said.

"But if we could," my girlfriend said and shook her head.

The saleswoman poured the last of the wine into our glasses. "The question you need to ask yourself," she said, "is how can you afford not to have a place like this?"

MY GIRLFRIEND EVENTUALLY left me for a man with an artificial leg, someone she'd met in her amputee support group. They'd been having an affair for months, pretty much the whole time I'd been dating her. She told me over breakfast one afternoon.

"What are we going to do now?" I asked, unbelieving.

"I don't know what *you're* going to do," she said, watching the fingers of her fake hand flex on the table, "but I know what *I'm* going to do."

"His cancer is going to come back, you know," I told her. "It's just growing somewhere else in his body right now."

"Well, if my mind wasn't made up about you before," she said.

"One day he's going to start having seizures because of a brain tumour or something. Where will you be then?"

Her hand spread itself out flat on the table and was still. She looked at me. "I won't be sitting here having this conversation with you," she said.

AFTER THAT I BEGAN spending all my spare time in movie theaters. There was one — a Cineplex Odeon with eight screens and Starbucks coffee — that I went back to over and over. It had air conditioning, and by the time I left my nose would be running, like I had a cold. Whenever one movie ended, I'd get up and go to the next one. Sometimes I'd come in halfway through it, sometimes it would be just beginning.

Once, a man in dress pants and a golf shirt sat right beside me. He held a bag of popcorn between his legs and asked me if I wanted any. I moved up several rows, and he didn't follow me.

Another time an usher woke me by shining a flashlight into my eyes. "You've been here all day," he said.

"I paid, I paid," I told him. I looked at the screen, but it was blank, the curtain drawn. There was no one else in the theatre.

"You paid for one show," he said. "You've been here all day." He was young, a teenager, with slicked-back hair and a thin moustache.

"I fell asleep."

"You have to leave before the next movie starts." He kept shining the flashlight in my eyes, even though the house lights were on.

"The place is empty," I said. "What difference does it make?"

"The difference is that you only paid for one show."

"Come on," I said. "Help a man out."

"Do you really want me to get the manager?" he asked.

BUT I HAVE TO tell you about what happened in the blind man's room.

We smoked a joint that tasted like cinnamon. He told me it was laced with a mild hallucinogen. "It's the only way I can see these days," he said.

We were sitting on his bed, and he'd taken his glasses off. He was staring at a spot two inches over my head. Now that I looked at him close, I could see his eyes were all scarred and the skin of his face pocked, like someone had taken a small knife to him. I was fully expecting him to make a pass at me, but he never did.

At some point in the night I asked him, "What kind of home is this?"

"What do you mean?"

"I mean, is everyone who lives here blind or deaf or something?"

"Oh yeah. But none of us were born this way, we were all normal once. You can't get in here unless you've been in an accident or something. Like the deaf guys. One of them blew his own eardrums out when he shot himself in the head."

"He shot himself in the head and he didn't die?"

"Yeah, it hit his skull and traveled around, went out the back. Never even touched his brain. But it made him deaf for some reason. The doctors couldn't explain it."

"What about the other one?" I asked.

"I don't know. It was some disease or something."

"Jesus," I said. "I had no idea there were places like this."

"You should see the people upstairs," he said. "Some of them can't even walk. They just lie in their rooms all day, watching television and talking to God, if they can even do that."

"I couldn't live like that," I told him.

"Maybe not," he said, "but what else can you do?"

There were no lamps in his room, but I could still see because there was light coming in through the window, from somewhere close. I got up and opened the blinds. The neighbouring house was only five or six feet away. I was looking into someone's kitchen. It was a big room, with an island in the center and stainless-steel pots hanging everywhere. It looked like an Ikea display. There was a woman sitting on the island, in between a wooden dish rack and a stack of magazines. Her skirt was pulled up around her hips, and a man was kneeling in front of her, his head and one of his hands between her thighs. She was looking right at me. I wasn't sure if they were really there or if I was just imagining them. Looking back on it now, I'm pretty sure I imagined them. But back then, I just didn't know.

"I think your neighbours are fucking," I told the blind man.

"You can see my neighbours?" He stood and came over to the window, turned his head from side to side.

The woman kept looking out her window but didn't seem to notice either one of us. She leaned back on one hand and ran the other through the man's hair. He had a bald spot at the back of his head.

"You can really see them?" he asked. "Where are they?"

"They're in the kitchen. They're fucking right there on the counter."

"Tell me what they look like," the blind man said. He had his hand on my arm again.

"She looks like the kind of woman you'd see on television," I said. "I don't know about him. I can't see his face because he's going down on her."

"Really?" He leaned forward, until his nose touched the glass.

"She's got her legs wrapped around his shoulders and everything," I told him.

"Wow. What are her tits like? Are they big?"

"I don't know, she's still dressed. She's just pulled up her skirt."

"But what do they look like? Do they look big?"

"They're all right, I guess."

"What about her panties?"

"I don't know. I can't see them. Maybe she wasn't wearing any."

"And her skirt?"

"It's a red floral thing. And a white shirt. Some sort of silk material."

"Oh yeah," he said. "I can see it."

The two of us stood there in silence for a moment, me watching this couple having sex, the blind guy staring in their direction and not seeing anything, or maybe seeing something only he could see, and the woman staring back at us. If she was even there at all.

She closed her eyes when she came. From this close, I could see the flush to her skin. The man stood up and grabbed a dishtowel from the counter, wiped his face with it. She hit him lightly on the shoulder and laughed as she hopped off the counter. They went out of the kitchen and didn't come back again. I never did see the man's face.

"Tell me what they're doing now," the blind man said when they were gone.

COULD I AFFORD YOU?

I WAS SITTING BESIDE an actor. We were talking to each other's reflections in the mirror behind the bar.

"I had an audition today," he told me. "They're going to pay me ten thousand dollars to be a body double." He shook his head like he was disappointed.

"What is it, some kind of stunt?" I asked.

"No, it's for this sex scene. You don't even get to see my face." He sipped his drink, some sort of martini, and sighed.

The bar was empty except for us and the one waitress working. It was two in the afternoon. He'd walked in and sat on the stool beside me, started talking like he was a friend of mine. He'd even bought me a beer. For that I had to listen to him.

"You should have seen the audition," he went on. "I thought it would be something personal, you know? Maybe me and the director in some locked room somewhere. A lot of talk about motivation and that kind of thing."

"Something intimate," I said.

"Exactly. Only it was nine fucking a.m. in this bright office, and there were two other people in there with him. The director of photography and some woman lawyer."

"Why'd they have a lawyer there?"

"I don't know. Something to do with lawsuits. Anyway, the audition consisted of me having to act the scene out. Only they made me do it with this blow-up doll instead of with a real person."

"You fucked a doll? With other people in the room?"

"No, no, I didn't fuck it. I acted like I was making love to it. It was an audition, remember?"

"I don't know," I said, "I don't think I could have done that."

"Oh, it wasn't so bad."

"Was it one of those lifelike dolls?" I asked. "The kind with the holes and everything?"

"You're missing the point here," he said.

WHEN I WASN'T working, I spent most of my time at The Code. It was one of those underground bars, the kind that no matter when you leave, you're always walking up into the light. The walls were covered in old movie posters. Bogart, Dean, Hepburn. It was always filled with beautiful people. There was some sort of modeling studio in the building upstairs and a Club Monaco across the street. The actor told me that all the movie stars drank there when they were in town. It was like I was living in L.A. or someplace like that.

The waitresses got to know me by name. They never charged me for more than six or seven drinks. One of them — she was Indian or Asian, I couldn't really tell — wanted to be a model, but she had a lazy eye, so she was never going to get any work. She called herself Mercedes, but I didn't think that was her real name. I was in love with her even though she was going out with the actor.

One night she sat with me at the bar after her shift was done. There was a man in a leather body suit a few stools down, drinking a Scotch. We all watched one of those medical shows on television. A team of surgeons was operating on a baby still in the womb. They cut open the mother and then cut open the baby inside her. They were playing Vivaldi in the operating room to keep the patients calm. There was something wrong with the baby's spine, but the announcer said it would be okay after the surgery.

"Imagine that," I said. "If someone fixed all your problems before you were born."

"Why wouldn't she just abort it and try again?" Mercedes asked.

"Just think about it," I told her. "What if someone had fixed your eye before anyone else had a chance to see it? Where would you be then?"

She lit a cigarette and looked at me through the smoke. "Why is it that you never go home?" she asked.

"What would I do there?"

"What do you do here?"

I turned back to the television. "The important thing," I said, "is that the baby is all right."

At some point in the night — I don't remember if it was before or after the surgery show — the man in the leather suit came over to us. "Would you like to come into the back room with me?" he asked Mercedes.

"I don't think so," she said.

"You don't have to do anything," he said. "You can just watch."

"Hey," I said, but neither one looked at me.

"I have a boyfriend," she said.

"Bring him along."

"Does your wife know you do this?"

"Married? I'm not married."

"I can see the ring mark on your finger." It was true — there was a thin band of scar tissue around his ring finger, as if he'd been married for years.

"Divorced," he said. "I can't even remember her name."

"That's what they all say," she said.

"How about if I pay you?" he asked. "Just to watch, like I said."

"You couldn't afford me."

"What about you?" he said, looking at me for the first time. "Could I afford you?"

THE CODE HAD a room in the back that was only for special events. The walls were painted black, and all the furniture was covered in white sheets. There were no windows. When there wasn't an event taking place, you could only get in with a key that was kept behind the bar. Sometimes the lights inside were red.

Every Monday there was a fetish party in the room. All night long people would walk in wearing leather or latex or even plastic. Sometimes men would show up in heels or fishnet stockings. Women with safety pins in their cheeks and arms. Once I saw a man leading a woman by a chain tied around her neck.

But mainly it was normal people, people in suits or dressed like you and me. They came in and had a drink or two at the counter and then changed in the washroom. When they came out they'd be wearing handcuffs or corsets or sometimes just leather underwear.

I wanted to look inside, to see what they did in there, but you had to pay ten dollars at the door. The man who'd asked Mercedes to go back there ran the parties and he stood outside the door most of the night with a little cash box. And the people inside all laughed and shouted at each other like they belonged there.

Once, though, no one at all showed up. It was raining so hard a storm sewer outside had overflowed, and water was trickling down the stairs into The Code. Mercedes was out with the actor. He'd picked her up after work, and the two of them had gone up into the storm, leaving me alone at the bar.

Now the man who ran the fetish nights — he later told me his name was Christopher, "like the saint" — was sitting beside me, drinking another Scotch. This time he wore leather pants with a mesh shirt that had no back. I could see his pierced nipples through the shirt. We were watching the television above the bar, but something was wrong with it — it kept flipping channels on its own, every few seconds.

"How come you haven't come to any of the parties yet?" Christopher wanted to know.

"It's not really my scene," I told him.

"You don't know until you try," he said.

"I don't think so."

The television finally seemed to settle on Discovery Channel, but then the screen went dead as the power went out. There was only the light of the candles to see by. I waited for the power to come back up but it didn't.

"Someone must have hit a line somewhere," Christopher said. "We'll probably be this way for a while."

I thought about going home and looked out the front door. It was raining harder than before. I didn't even own an umbrella.

"We could go back there now," he said. "While we're waiting."

I pulled a couple of candles closer and didn't say anything, just looked up at the dead television.

"I won't even charge you."

THE AIR IN THE back room smelled like it had been in there for years. All the couches and chairs had been pulled up against the walls, and the fetish gear filled the center of the room. There were large wooden crosses you tied people to, and benches for kneeling on, and padded handcuffs hanging from the ceiling beams.

"Try anything you want," Christopher said. He leaned against one of the crosses and watched me.

"I'm just looking," I said.

"There's more in the corner," he said, pointing at a stack of boxes.

There was everything inside them — crumpled leather gloves, plastic balls with straps attached, wooden paddles. I put on a zippered face mask with no mouth hole, only openings for the nose and eyes. It tasted of salt.

"It's you," Christopher said.

Another box held a collection of whips. I pulled up the mask so I could speak. "What are these for?" I asked.

"What do you think they're for?"

I took out a short whip with a dozen leather straps the length of my forearm and snapped it through the air a couple of times. "You don't actually hit each other with these things, do you?"

"Why don't you give it a try?" he asked.

"I don't think so," I said. "I'm not that way."

"Just once," he said. "You might like it." He turned around and spread himself against the rack. The bare skin of his back looked golden in the candlelight. I walked up behind him but didn't do anything. "I can't," I said.

"I don't mind."

I hit him with the whip as hard as I could. It made the same kind of noise as punches do in movies. I was surprised to see blood on his skin right away.

"Jesus Christ!" He jumped away from me and stumbled over one of the benches, fell to the floor. "You fucking maniac!"

"What?" I asked. "You said I could."

"Not that fucking hard," he shouted. He felt around behind his back and then showed me his bloody fingertips. "Look at that! I'm going to need a doctor now!"

"Maybe they have a first aid kit here," I said.

"What the fuck is wrong with you?"

"But isn't this what you all do in here?" I asked.

The only waitress working came to the door and stopped.

"Do you know where the first aid kit is?" I asked.

She looked at me standing there with the whip and the mask, looked at Christopher writhing on the floor, and then she closed the door.

SOMETIMES THE PEOPLE from the modeling studio upstairs used the room for shoots. It would always be one man — the photographer — and a group of women. They'd come in and get the key from whatever waitress was working and lock themselves in there. Sometimes they wouldn't come out for hours. I imagined them having sex in there, on the couches or maybe on piles of the clothes they brought in with them, like a scene out of some movie.

One night I helped with a shoot. A photographer came in with three models from upstairs. None of the women looked over eighteen, but one of them paid for a round of drinks with a gold card. They sat at the booth underneath the Hepburn poster and smoked cigars all night long. They were sitting in the No Smoking section, but the waitress working that night — a new woman I didn't know, who charged me full price for the drinks — never said anything to them.

Around midnight, the photographer came over to the bar, where I'd been sitting all night. "You work here?" he asked. I looked around for the waitress, but she was nowhere in sight.

"Yeah," I said. "I work here."

"We're ready for the back room now," he said.

I wasn't exactly sure what he meant, but I went around the counter and got the key anyway. When I opened the door, the models all wandered into the room and sat down on the furniture there. Each of them carried a couple of garment bags that they dropped to the floor once they were inside. "I could use a glass of water," one of them said. She held her foot up to look at her toenails. I went back to the bar and poured some water into a glass, threw a lemon slice from a bowl into it, and brought it to her. She took it without saying thanks or even looking at me.

The photographer had taken the sheets off the fetish equipment and was looking at it all. "We need this stuff brought out and, um, arranged," he said.

"All right." I dragged the wooden crosses out to where he pointed and turned them around under the lights until he told me to stop. The models watched in silence. One of them fell asleep for a while.

"That's enough," the photographer eventually said to me. I let go of the aluminum cage I'd pushed out of one of the corners and stood next to him, like I was his assistant or something. "Why don't we start with that black vest thing?" he said to one of the women. She nodded and stood up, started to take off her shirt. She had on a black lace bra underneath.

"What kind of shoot is this?" I asked. I imagined seeing this room and these models on bus ads, or maybe even billboards.

"It's nothing like that," the photographer said. "These are just, ah, audition photos."

The model opened up one of the garment bags and took out a sleeveless leather vest, put it on. It zipped up to her throat. The photographer pushed her against one of the crosses. "Could you hold her hands?" he asked. I thought he meant me and I started to step forward, but he was talking to one of the other models. She walked around behind the cross and held the first one's wrists. The third one took a cell phone out of her pocket and started talking on it. "I won't be making class tomorrow," she said. "Can you take notes for me?"

"Maybe one of those balls in her mouth," the photographer said, and this time he looked at me.

I went over to the boxes and searched through them until I found what he wanted, a red plastic ball with a leather head strap attached. "You want me to put it on her?" I asked.

Just then the waitress came in. "What are you doing in here?" she asked.

"We're working," I said.

"What are you talking about?" she asked. "You don't work here."

Everyone looked at me.

"It's just for tonight," I said.

"No," she said, "you don't work here."

The photographer took the mouthpiece from my hands. "Maybe you should lock the door," he said to the waitress.

"Oh, come *on*," I said.

NOW IT WAS THE day after that incident and I was sitting alone at the bar again, watching television. Someone drove a Volvo off a cliff. A group of men and women in white lab coats watched. The sky was a shade of blue I'd never seen before. There was a quick close-up of the driver of the car, screaming as it fell down toward the ground.

"Isn't that your boyfriend?" I asked Mercedes.

"I don't have a boyfriend," she said.

The camera cut to the wrecked car at the bottom of the cliff. It looked like it had been run through a crusher. Then the door opened and the driver stepped out, waved at the men and women in lab coats. The Volvo logo appeared on the screen.

"Yeah, that's your boyfriend," I said.

She looked at the television. "I don't know who that is," she said.

BUT HE CAME in that very afternoon. He stood beside me and leaned against the bar. He was wearing a silver Rolex that looked new. Mercedes was sitting at the end of the bar, smoking a cigarette and reading a *Vogue*. "What do you want?" she asked him.

"I want my videos back," he said.

"Not the ones I'm in," she said. "No way."

"I don't want those," he said. "I want the *films*."

"Fine. You can have those."

"I know I can have them. They're mine."

"I'll drop them off on the weekend."

"All right." He sat down beside me and tossed a gold card on the counter. "In the meantime I want a latte."

"I'm not serving you."

He looked at his reflection in the mirror. "I want a latte. With cinnamon."

"You hear that?" Mercedes said to me. "He wants a latte."

"I don't hear anything," I said.

He turned to look at me. "Who the fuck are you," he asked, "to talk to me?"

I looked at Mercedes, but she just kept on reading the *Vogue*. I reached behind the counter and grabbed the key, went to the back room. I emptied the boxes onto the floor until I found one of the whips. Then I went back into the main room.

Mercedes and the actor both laughed when they saw me. "What do you think you're going to do with that?" he asked.

I stopped behind him. "The lady asked you to leave," I said, meeting his gaze in the mirror.

"All right," Mercedes said. "I think this has gone far enough."

"Is this what you've been reduced to?" the actor asked, looking at her. "The lady? You sorry cunt."

I hit him with the whip. I was careful not to hit him hard, but the leather straps still made a sound like a slap.

"Hey," he said. He covered his face with his hands, even though I hit him on the back. "Hey hey hey HEY!"

I kept hitting him. He got off the stool and ran toward the door, and I followed him. Mercedes was laughing even harder now, and I started laughing myself. "Who's the cunt now?" I asked. "Huh? Who's the cunt now?"

THE RAIN HAD FINALLY stopped, and now I was sitting beside a table of three women who looked like secretaries. One of them was wearing a red silk blindfold, even though it wasn't a fetish night. A sign made of red construction paper hung from a string around her neck. It said, Kiss Me, I'm Getting Married. The others already wore wedding bands. There was no one else in the place.

Mercedes had stopped coming to work. I went to The Code every day for a week, sometimes staying six or eight hours, but she never showed up again. None of the other waitresses knew what had happened to her. That's what they told me, anyway.

"When are you getting married?" I asked the blindfolded woman.

"Next month," one of the other women said. She had blond hair that was black at the roots.

"Well, you've got plenty of time to live a little then."

"That's what we're doing," the blond-haired woman said. They were all smiling and pushing their gold bracelets up and down their arms.

"You know what I mean," I said.

"No, we don't," she said, but she was laughing when she said it.

I went over to the bar and ordered a round of martinis from the waitress, the one who charged me full price for everything. "Put it on my tab," I told her.

"You don't have a tab," she said. "But I can put it on your bill."

"That'll be fine," I said.

"How are you going to pay for all this?" she asked me.

"I have three credit cards," I told her.

"Maybe you should give me one now. Just to make sure."

Back at the table, I asked the blindfolded woman what her husband did.

"We're not married yet," she said. It was the first time I'd heard her speak. She sounded like she'd been drinking for some time before they came in here.

"What's your boyfriend do then?" I asked.

"He's a lawyer," she said.

"A *corporate* lawyer," the blond-haired woman put in.

"A lawyer?" I said. "That the best you can do?"

"What about you?" the third woman asked. She had a huge purple blemish on her cheek, like she'd been burned or punched hard. "What do *you* do?"

"Me? I'm a doctor."

"A doctor."

"That's right."

"What's your specialty, doc?"

"I fix kids."

When the martinis came, the two women who could see just stared at them. "We didn't order these," the blond-haired woman said.

"What are they?" the blindfolded woman asked.

"They're from him," the waitress said, nodding in my direction. The secretaries all turned their heads my way for a moment.

"To marriage," I said.

They sipped the martinis and started talking about something to do with the wedding — the colour of the dresses or the flowers or something like that. I got up and went to the washroom.

When I came out, only the blindfolded woman was sitting at the table, alone with the half-finished martinis. The others were at the bar, ordering more drinks. I stopped and stood beside their table for a moment.

The blindfolded woman turned her head in my direction, like she sensed me there. I bent down beside her. She licked her lips, flattened her hands on the table. For a moment I just looked at her, watching the way she strained against the silk covering her eyes. Then I kissed her gently, just brushing my lips against hers. I could taste mint on her breath. She put her hand on my chest. We only went on that way for a second or two, but it was like we had been lovers for years.

THIS ISN'T WHAT I WANTED

DURING SOME OF THIS TIME, I worked in a call center. It was the kind of place you see on television — all pink cubicles and windowless walls. I worked the night shift, taking roadside assistance calls. It was the only job the temp agency could find for me.

People phoned me for help all night long. The woman who trained me — an older woman who wore bifocals and whose name was actually Hope — told me to always act like I cared about their problems. "Ask them if they're all right first," she said. "Then make sure their membership is still valid." She told me she'd been a social worker before this.

"And what if their membership's not valid?" I asked.

"Then you don't have to pretend to care anymore," she said. "Get them off the line."

"But what if they're in real trouble?" I wanted to know. "What if they're lying in a ditch somewhere, pinned inside the car while water rises all around them?"

"Then you're the last person they should be calling for help," she said.

BUT SOMETIMES PEOPLE did call when they were in real trouble. Once, a woman started screaming that she was on fire before I could even say anything.

"Are you all right?" I asked, remembering what Hope had told me.

"I just said I'm on fire," she shrieked. "Does that sound all right to you?"

"What part of you is on fire?" I asked. "Is it your clothes? If it's your clothes, just take them off."

"My *car*," she said. "My car is on fire." I could hear a horn go off in the background, and what sounded like a child's laughter.

"Shouldn't you be calling 911 or someone like that?" I asked.

"I did, I did," she said. "But I need all the help I can get here."

"All right," I said. "I just need your membership number."

"My membership number?" I could hear a car alarm going off now. "It's ... Don't you even want to know where I am?"

"I need the number first," I told her. "I have to enter everything into the computer in the right order."

"My car is on fire," she shouted, "and you're talking to me about order?"

"There's nothing I can do," I told her. "It's the system."

Her voice faded. "Don't worry about the damned groceries," I heard her yell at someone. "The car is going to blow up!"

"I don't think cars actually blow up," I said. "I think that's only in the movies."

"What are you saying?" she asked, back now. "Are you telling me my car is not blowing up?"

"I'm just saying I think that's only in the movies."

"I wish *this* was a movie."

MOSTLY, THOUGH, it was just sending out tow trucks for cars with dead batteries or empty gas tanks. During storms, the calls were back to back, all night long. I couldn't take a break until it slowed down, because the system automatically routed waiting calls to me. When I did get a break, I had to sign out of my computer. The router stopped sending me calls for exactly ten minutes, after which it started up again whether I was in my cubicle or not.

Once, I came back to my cubicle late and found the phone ringing and my supervisor, Adam, sitting in my chair, feet up on the desk. His eyes were closed, and he was wearing a special headset that let him listen to anyone's call without them knowing. He was twenty-two but already going bald.

"I don't know what you did before this," he told me, still not opening his eyes, "but you can't do it here."

"I was only two minutes late," I said.

"Every time you're late, you get docked an hour's pay. It's automatic."

"That's not really fair," I said.

He only opened his eyes when he got out of my chair and stretched. His back made cracking noises, and I could hear distant voices coming from his headset. "It has nothing to do with fair," he said. "It has to do with the system."

NONE OF THE CALLERS knew we could listen to them when we put them on hold. Sometimes I did it just to hear what they would say. Once I heard a man with a dead battery threaten his girlfriend. "When we get out of this," he said, "I am going to fuck you up so bad." I could hear her laugh in the background.

"No," he said, "I mean it." But she kept on laughing.

Another man, this one with a flat tire, seemed to be having sex with someone. As soon as I put him on hold he started moaning. "Mmm," he said, *"God!"*

I came back on the line. "Everything all right?" I asked.

"Everything except the car," he said, his voice back to normal.

"Just checking," I said and put him on hold once more.

"Don't stop," he groaned.

AND I HAD A regular caller, a man named Jude. The first time he called, he told me he'd run out of gas. The info on the computer said he was from Yellowknife. "How's the weather up there?" I asked him as I filled in the forms on the screen. Hope said to always keep people talking. If they were talking, they weren't wondering what you were doing.

"Oh, it's not so bad," Jude said. "No worse than usual, anyway."

I looked up at the television mounted in one corner of the office. It was always tuned to one of the weather channels, and right now it was showing the entire state covered in a snowstorm.

"How long do you think it'll take to get someone out here?" he asked.

"Depends on how many other people are broken down," I said.

"Because I need to find my girlfriend," he said.

"Maybe you should call her and let her know you're going to be late," I said.

"No, no," he said, "I have to *find* her. She hasn't been home in two days, and I really don't know where she is."

"Well, that's not really our business," I said.

"I don't know what to do," he went on. "She's usually only gone the night."

"Have you tried calling the police?" I asked.

"The police." He laughed. "What are they going to do?"

I finished the forms and asked him where to send the driver with the gas. He gave me the address, and I paused as I looked at the screen.

"Isn't that your home address?" I asked.

"That's right," he said.

"You ran out of gas at home?" I asked.

"Well, technically it happened down the street a bit," he said, "but I managed to get her back in the driveway before she really gave out on me."

"Is there anything else I can help you with?" I asked.

"I don't know," he said. There was a silence, like he was waiting for me to say something.

"Well, good luck with this girlfriend thing," I said.

"It's not luck I need," he said.

HOPE SAT IN THE cubicle next to mine. Every shift she received an obscene call. "It's always the same guy," she told me one night while we were waiting for the computers to come back up after a system crash. "He never says anything, but I know."

"How can you tell it's him if he doesn't say anything?" I asked.

"He always comes at the same time," she said. She tapped her watch. "Sixty seconds, that's all it takes."

"He comes when he's talking to you?"

"I can tell by the breathing," she said. "You know, it starts off slow and quiet, and then, wham, it's like he's dying."

"And you listen to this?" I asked. "Why don't you disconnect?"

She shrugged. "It's only sixty seconds out of my day," she said. "And it's a break from the regular type of calls." She leaned back in her chair and folded her hands on her lap, stared at her blank screen. "But I can't tell you how glad I am I wasn't born with a penis."

Once, she let me listen to him. I'd just come back from a break, and she waved me over. I plugged my headset into the extra jack on her phone base in time to hear this man gasping like he was running a marathon or something.

"Hello?" Hope said. "Is anyone there?"

The man made choking noises.

"Can I help you?" Hope asked, smiling at me. He let out a long sigh, and she pointed at her watch. "Hello?" she said again and kept repeating it until we heard the dial tone.

I unplugged my headset from her phone. "How does he keep getting you?" I asked. "I thought the calls were all routed automatically."

"They are," she said. "So I don't think it's coming from outside."

"What do you mean?" I asked.

"It's someone in here," she said, looking around the room. There were maybe a dozen men scattered around the cubicles. "But at least now I know it's not you."

I ONLY RECEIVED one obscene call during the time I was there. It was around three or four in the morning, the quiet time. "Bitch," the man whispered after I answered. "Slut."

"Hey," I said. "You're talking to a man."

"Tell me what you're wearing," he went on. "I want to know what you look like." I could hear soft slapping noises in the background.

"I've got an obscene call," I said to Hope.

"It's not my guy, is it?" she asked, frowning.

"Put me on the speaker phone," he gasped.

"No, this one talks," I told her.

"You cunt," he sobbed.

"What if someone was really in trouble?" I said to him. "What if their car was on fire and they were trying to call right now, but couldn't get through because of you?"

"*That's it*," he moaned and came.

JUDE CALLED ME two more times. The first time, his voice was low and thick, as if he was thinking about each word. "I was hoping you were working tonight," he said.

"How did you get me again?" I asked.

"I just kept trying until you answered," he said. "It only took three times."

"Why me?" I asked.

"I thought we developed a rapport the other night," he said. He pronounced the "t" in "rapport."

"Well, what can I do for you this time?" I asked.

"Dead battery," he said. "I need a boost."

"Your car in the driveway again?" I asked.

"It's a truck," he said. "And yeah, it is."

"All right," I said. I started on the forms. "How's the weather tonight?"

"It's getting worse," he said. "I don't think I'm going to be able to make it to work."

I looked up at the television. The weather channel was predicting sunshine for Yellowknife all week.

"All right, I'll send someone right away," I said.

"That'd be great," he said. There was a sound like ice clinking in a glass, and then he said, "I couldn't find her. She still hasn't come back."

"Who hasn't come back?" I asked.

"My girlfriend," he said. "It's been a week now."

"I don't think this is something I can help you with," I said.

"But she did call," he went on.

"Well, what more do you want?" I asked.

"She doesn't think it's working out between us," he said. "Now what am I supposed to do?"

"Have you tried asking her what the problem is?" I said.

"Oh yeah," he said. "She said she wasn't really sure. It was just a feeling she had. What am I supposed to say to that?"

"Maybe it's time to move on," I said.

"No, I can't do that," he said. "I just to need to repair this, uh, situation."

"I don't see why you're telling me all of this," I said.

"You talk to people all the time for your job, right?" he said.

"Yes ..." I said.

"So you're good with communicating."

"I mainly dispatch tow trucks," I told him. "That doesn't require too much communication."

"And you help people," he said. "That's exactly the combination I need."

"I don't understand," I said.

"I'll get her back here," he said, "and we'll call you. Then you can talk to her. And you'll fix everything for us. Right?"

I didn't say anything for a moment.

"Right?" he said again.

"Sure," I said.

"You'll take care of us?"

"I'll take care of you," I said.

When the call was done, Adam came on the line. "What," he said, "was that?"

I looked around but couldn't see him anywhere.

"This is a call center," he said, "not a distress line."

"What could I do?" I said.

"You could have told him to call back only if had a real problem. You could have not said you'd help him talk to his girlfriend."

"That was just to get rid of him."

"If he does call back, I want you to hang up on him."

"All right," I said.

"Or we'll be hanging up on you."

AND ONCE I HAD a suicide call. Before I could even say anything, the woman on the other end said, "I'm going to kill myself."

"You have the wrong number," I told her. "This is for people whose cars have broken down."

"I'm sitting in my car," she said. "I've got a knife. And a whole bottle of sleeping pills."

"Is there anything wrong with the car?" I asked her.

"*I'm* broken," she said. "I'm going to kill myself."

"So there's nothing wrong with the car," I said.

"No," she said. "The car is fine. I just had it tuned up, in fact. I'm driving it around as we speak."

"Well, what do you want from me then?" I asked.

"I want you to listen."

I looked up, across the room, and saw Adam standing outside his office, gazing around the floor. He was wearing his headset but he wasn't looking at me. I disconnected and went outside for a break.

Hope was standing on the stairs outside the building, smoking a cigarette. I told her about the suicide call.

"They always want you to listen," she said and shook her head.

"I'm not trained for this," I said.

"I wouldn't worry about it," she told me. "It's best never to believe anything these people say."

"So you don't think she was going to kill herself?"

"Well, what would you be able to do about it if she was?" She shook her head again. "No, it's really best not to believe them."

THE LAST TIME Jude called was the night I was fired. "I couldn't get her to come back here," he said, "so I'm just going to call her on my cell phone and we'll do it that way."

"You can't keep calling like this," I said.

"I can tell you what she says," he went on, "or I can just put the two phones together and you can talk to her directly. Whatever works for you."

"What works for me is hanging up right now," I said.

"But you're here to help me," he said. "It says so right on my membership card."

"Goodbye," I told him.

"I locked my baby in the truck," he said quickly.

I paused but didn't say anything.

"The truck's still running," he said. "In the garage. It's going to fill up with carbon monoxide."

"Why don't you just open the garage door," I said.

"It's stuck," he said. "Frozen solid. You have to help me."

"Don't do this," I told him.

"If you hang up on me," he said, "you'll be killing my baby."

"Do you even have a baby?" I asked.

"It's ours," he said. "Me and my girlfriend's."

I didn't say anything for a moment, and he took my silence for assent, started giving me the information I needed. By the time I was done filling out the forms on the computer, I could hear a distant ringing. "I'm just calling her now," he said, his voice distant. I realized he had put the phones up against each other and was listening in on both.

But there was no answer. The phone kept ringing and ringing. There wasn't even voice mail. "All right," I said after a minute or so of this. "You have to stop."

"Can we call her back later?" Jude asked.

"Yeah, we can call her back later," I said.

"I'll tell her to buy an answering machine," he said. "So you can leave a message if she's not there."

"All right," I said. "Sure."

"Great," he said.

"Someone will be there shortly to get your baby out of the truck," I said.

"Right, right," he said and hung up.

Adam came on the line right away. "You can start packing up your things now," he said.

I didn't even bother looking around for him. "What else could I do?" I said.

"I don't know," he said.

"Did you listen to the whole call?" I asked.

"Yeah."

"Then why didn't you say something earlier?" I asked. "Why didn't you just disconnect the call?"

"It wasn't my call," he said. "It was yours."

"Do you think there really was a baby?" I asked.

"I don't know," he said. There was only dead air for a moment, and then he said, "It's nothing personal."

OUTSIDE, HOPE WAS standing on the steps of the building, smoking a cigarette. I told her what had happened. She looked at me for a moment, then up at the sky. It was beginning to rain again. I couldn't see the moon anywhere.

"You got fired over someone you don't even know?" Hope asked.

"I sort of knew him," I said.

She took one last drag on the cigarette and then dropped it to the ground. "I hope he doesn't call me next."

"He just needs someone to talk to," I said.

Hope nodded, then said, "Well, I'd better get back inside. Someone's going to have to take all your calls now." But she paused halfway in there, holding the door open as she looked back at me. "I never talk to them myself," she said. "But I've been doing this a lot longer than you."

I didn't say anything, just looked at her. She closed the door and disappeared back into the building, leaving me alone there.

"All right," I said and went down the steps. "It's all right."

PLEASE

I MET THE COMA WOMAN at Kennedy's place. I went there to talk to him about a job, but he was throwing a party when I drove up. People were staggering out of his yard and falling down in the street. I drove around them and parked a dozen houses up, then walked back, holding my jacket over my head to protect myself from the rain. Two weeks of it had turned all the lawns into swamps and still it came down, filling the air like static. At the end of Kennedy's driveway, two women were trying to lift a man who was lying face down in the street, his head half-submerged in the overflow from a storm drain. "He's going to drown," one of the women kept saying, but the other was laughing so hard they couldn't even get his face out of the water.

Kennedy was sitting on the swing set in the front yard, smoking a joint with a woman who held an umbrella above them. For some reason he was wearing a housecoat over his jeans and T-shirt. "Hey, glad you could make it," he said and offered me the joint. He kept holding it out to me even after I shook my head.

"I didn't know you were having a party," I said.

"It's to celebrate my new job," he said.

"You didn't invite me," I said.

"I didn't?"

"Wyman told me you had a line on a job. I came here to talk to you about that. I didn't know anything about a party."

"*I* got a job," Kennedy said. "I don't have anything for you."

Beside him, the woman reached out and took the joint from his hand, then disappeared under the umbrella.

The rain was starting to seep through my jacket, which I was still holding over my head. Kennedy kept on grinning at me, but he had to blink against the rain hitting his eyes. Finally, he said, "Well, the important thing is that you're here now."

WE WENT UP the stairs to his apartment and into the kitchen, where half a dozen men and women were playing cards at the table. They all looked at me for a moment and then went back to staring at their cards. I didn't know any of them. Kennedy took a pair of Heinekens from the fridge and handed me one. "It's all that's left," he apologized.

"Those are mine," said one of the card players, a man with dreadlocks and a beard. He hadn't looked away from his cards.

I turned to Kennedy, but he'd already wandered off into the living room.

"Help yourself," the other man said. He threw out the jack of spades and kept staring at his hand. "I just want you to know they're mine."

THERE WERE ANOTHER dozen or so people in the living room, talking in the corners or dancing in the middle of the room. All the furniture had been pushed to the walls. The music was coming from speakers taped to the ceiling fan with duct tape. The television was on in one corner of the room, showing the aftermath of some bombing somewhere, but the sound was muted. Kennedy and I sat on the couch, beside the coma woman. I thought she was only sleeping at first, but she didn't wake up when I pushed her legs aside, just moaned a little and wrapped her arms tighter around the cushion she was hugging. It looked like she'd been drooling into it heavily for some time.

"That's Mia," Kennedy said. "King brought her."

"King's here?" I looked around the room but I didn't seem to know anyone here. "I think he was the one who stole my Tom Waits tickets."

"He was here," Kennedy said, "but then he had to go work a party somewhere."

"Took them right out of my wallet."

"And he just left her here," Kennedy went on. "Without telling me. What am I supposed to do with her?"

I looked at Mia. She was wearing cheap camouflage pants and a black hooded sweatshirt, but the Swatch on her wrist looked real. "Is she his girlfriend?" I asked.

"I don't know," Kennedy answered. "I thought so at first, but then she kept going on about her dead boyfriend."

"Dead?"

"Electrocuted. Got zapped by a faulty mike."

"He was a singer?"

"I think so," Kennedy said. "Either that or a roadie. She told me, but I can't remember exactly." He shook his head. "She keeps his ashes on her bedside table."

"Now that's love," I said.

"It's certainly something," Kennedy said. He drained half the Heineken in one swallow, then smacked his lips. "King's always leaving his shit here. It's got to stop."

We watched a trio of women dance in the center of the room for a while. Their clothes were all wet, so they'd stripped down to just pants and bras, but even their skin looked cold and white. "Who are these people?" I asked.

"I have no idea," Kennedy said. "They came with some people from the new job. But everyone I knew left a long time ago."

We watched the women for a moment longer, and then I said, "What kind of job is this anyway?"

"It's a broker kind of thing," he said.

"What do you know about being a broker?" I asked.

"It's not what you know," he said, "it's what you act like you know."

He finished the Heineken and dropped the bottle to the floor, then he got up and started dancing with the women. They opened their circle just enough that he could get in but they didn't speak to him. He didn't seem to mind.

I got up and went into the kitchen. The card players were all half-undressed now, a pile of clothes on one side of the table. I tried to find my shoes. They weren't where I had left them. "I think someone took my shoes," I said.

"What exactly are you trying to say?" the man with the dreadlocks asked, looking at me.

I went back to searching for my shoes in the muddy pile without answering him. I was still looking for them when Kennedy dragged Mia into the kitchen. She was still unconscious. "Do me a favour, man," he said, shoving her at me. "Take her with you."

She was boneless, arms and legs flopping, eyes rolling sightlessly. I pushed her right back. "She's not mine, I don't want her."

"You brought your car, though. You can take her in that."

For the next few seconds we bounced her back and forth between us, the card players watching silently, until her head slammed into my jaw. I caught her in my arms before she hit the floor, but only just. Then Kennedy pushed us out the door, and we fell down the stairs. My head hit the rail, and everything slid to one side for a moment. When it came back, I was lying on the wet ground outside. Far above my head, the moon glowed through the clouds.

When I sat up, there was wet newspaper clinging to my arms and legs. I tried pulling it off but it only came away in little strips. I pushed myself to my feet and started off toward the street. The woman with the umbrella was still pushing herself back and forth on the swing set, watching me now. I remembered Mia and went back for her. She was lying face down in the muck, still unconscious. Her head rolled like her neck was broken when I picked her up, but her breathing was regular at least. I carried her to my car and dropped her on the hood while I looked for my keys. The rain really came down then, knocking me sideways while I unlocked the doors. I jammed Mia into the passenger seat and covered her with an old blanket I kept in the back. I had no idea what I was going to do with her.

When I walked around to the driver's side, I noticed an old couple standing a few cars down, watching me. They were wearing dark jogging suits with reflective stripes and shining white running shoes, and their hair was plastered to their heads, like they'd been out in the rain all night. When they saw me looking at them, they slowly jogged away, glancing back over their shoulders every now and then.

I got in the car and started it. "Hotel California" was playing on the radio, and I reached for the tuning knob before I remembered it had broken off last week. I slammed my hand into the radio until it stopped, then sat there for a long moment, watching the windshield fog up from my breath. Our wet clothes made the car smell like some animal.

The clock in the dashboard said it was one in the morning. What were those people doing running in the rain at one in the morning?

I DROVE BLINDLY around the streets for maybe five minutes, shivering and watching my skin turn white from the street lamps. I didn't know where to go.

"Maybe I should just take you to a hospital," I said to Mia. "What do you think of that?" She didn't answer, didn't even move under the blanket.

I looked out the window, at the dark houses surrounding us. We were in a neighbourhood I'd never seen before. Quiet little houses from the fifties, old trees, children's bicycles left in the front yards. No garbage in sight anywhere. I had no idea where I was.

"There must be a hospital around here somewhere," I said.

I STOPPED AT a 7-Eleven for directions. It took forever to get from the car to the doors, the rain beating down on me the whole time like a million tiny fists.

It was as spotless as a commercial inside, everything in neat rows on the shelves, air freshener instead of air. The only sign of life was a thin trail of brownish water leading to the coffeepot. Behind the counter, a man of about forty or so was eating a potato chips and flipping channels on a miniature television set. I saw the same bombing scene I'd seen at Kennedy's place, before he switched it to the end of 2001.

"I need to find a hospital," I told him, counting out pocket change for a coffee.

"It's not that bad," he said. "All you need is a bandage."

"What are you talking about?" I asked.

He touched his lips and pointed at me but didn't say anything.

I raised a hand to my mouth and watery blood ran down my fingers. There was a small gash in my lower lip. "Jesus," I said. "When did that happen?"

"I wouldn't know," he said, turning back to the television. "But the bandages are in the third aisle, middle top shelf."

"I don't have time for that," I said. "I've got a woman in a coma outside."

He gave me the directions, but only after I paid for the coffee.

THE HOSPITAL'S emergency room smelled like soap. The place was nearly empty when I carried Mia inside, just one couple and their kids sitting in a circle in the corner. The parents glanced up at us, then went back to praying quietly. The kids stared at the floor the whole time.

I dropped Mia into a chair at the nurses' station and waited. Behind the glass wall in front of me, three nurses were talking about their various ex-husbands. It sounded like the same guy to me. I was still waiting for them to figure this out when one of them came over and asked, "What's the problem?"

"No problem," I said. "I just want to drop her off." We both looked at Mia. A string of drool slowly slipped from her chin to her chest.

"Has she been drinking?" the nurse asked.

"I'm not really sure," I said.

The nurse looked back at me. "You're not really sure? Now what does that mean?"

"I don't know," I said. "I found her. I thought maybe I could leave her here."

"Sure, we'll just have to fill out the paperwork for that," the nurse said. She smiled at the other nurses when she said it, and I couldn't tell if she was joking or not. She had me go through Mia's pockets, but all I could find was a piece of paper with an address written on it. Five Crossings. I couldn't find her ID anywhere.

The nurse entered my name and address on a form, then took us down the hall to another room. What seemed like hours later, an old, red-faced doctor finally came in. He glanced at Mia and then washed his hands in the sink.

"You the father or the boyfriend?" he asked.

"Neither," I said. "I've only just met her." I couldn't take my eyes off the garbage can in the corner. It was full of bloody bandages. I wondered what had gone on in there before we'd arrived.

"She been drinking?" the doctor asked.

"That's what the nurse figured."

He shone a light in Mia's eyes and felt her pulse for a moment. "You have pieces of newspaper stuck all over you," he told me through a yawn.

"Yes, I know that," I said.

"You also have no shoes on," he pointed out.

"I know that, too, thanks."

"Well, she'll probably be all right," he said, dropping Mia's hand. "She just needs to sleep it off. Now let's have a look at that lip and we can get you two on your way."

"I want to leave her here, though," I said.

"You can't do that," he said. "There's really nothing wrong with her."

"But I don't want her."

"This isn't the pound."

IT WAS STILL RAINING when I took Mia back to the car. I dropped her in the passenger seat and sat there for a moment, wondering what to do next. I looked at the piece of paper with the address again, then searched for the map in the glove compartment. I had to sort through a mess of candy wrappers, condoms, Wake-Ups, a bag of chips I couldn't remember buying, and the registration papers — so faded and water-stained I couldn't even read them any more — before I found it. Crossings Street was at the farthest edge of the city, an area I'd never been to before.

"King had better be there," I told Mia, then started up the car.

WHEN I FINALLY found Crossings Street, it was only a half-built subdivision. A few of the houses were finished, but most were still empty frames. You could have seen the stars through them, if you could actually see the stars anywhere around here.

Five Crossings was one of the biggest houses I'd ever seen.

Two long storeys of swirling stone and glass walls rising up out of a muddy lot. Practically a mansion.

I parked the car on the empty street, under a street lamp that kept turning on and off, and carried Mia to the door. I knocked but no one answered. I thought about leaving her on the doorstep. Then I tried the door. It was open. No alarms went off. I stepped inside.

For a moment, I thought I'd walked into a church. It was dark inside, but there was enough light from the street lamp that I could see the place was empty, just one cavernous room after another. But the walls. The walls were covered with giant murals of angels falling from white clouds, toward buildings in ruins beneath them. It was only when I walked into the next room and saw the murals there — Charles Manson, Margaret Thatcher, Burt Reynolds, all dancing together around a bonfire — that I realized it was all spray paint. Graffiti.

I dragged Mia through two living rooms and into the kitchen. There were no appliances in here, just empty spaces in the walls. It didn't look like anybody had ever lived here. There was no sound but our breathing.

I looked out the back window. There was a huge yard but no grass. It was all mud. And there was a large hole that looked as if it might have been made for a pool that had never been put in, or had been put in and taken away.

I found some stairs leading to the second floor and carried Mia up them. All the rooms up here were empty too. I took her into a bedroom bigger than my entire apartment and locked the door behind us.

I lowered Mia to the floor and then lay down beside her. I thought about my stolen Tom Waits tickets again. When Mia started to moan and shiver, I took off her wet sweatshirt. The alternating light from the street lamp made everything look like snapshots. I could see her bra had little kissing Mickey and Minnie

Mouse figures all over it. I thought about taking it off as well, but then she sighed and rolled into me, slipped her hand around my waist.

I looked at her a moment longer, then took off my jacket, the inside of which was still more or less dry, and wrapped it around her. I could feel her breath against my chest. I laid my head back on the polished hardwood floor and closed my eyes.

I DREAMED ABOUT my wife, Rachel, there. Only it was more a memory than a dream. We were in another rainstorm, years earlier. We were swimming in this luxury condo's outdoor pool. We'd just been driving by when we saw it. No one was in it. We parked the car and climbed over the fence, took off our clothes. It was sometime past midnight. Sheets of lightning fell from the sky. Rachel stood on the diving board, naked, her arms held up to the sky like she was calling it down. And then an old woman came out onto a balcony above us and shouted, "Get out of here! You don't belong here!"

"Yes, we do," Rachel shouted back. "This is all ours!"

"I've called the police," the old woman said.

"This is where we live," Rachel said. And then she dove in and came to me under the water, pulling me down to her.

I WOKE TO the sounds of glass breaking in the distance and an engine starting up. For a moment I thought my car was being stolen. Then I heard something louder, something collapsing. I got up and went to the window.

Outside, the rain had finally stopped, and the early morning air had become a thin mist. My car was still there, its windows unbroken. The neighbouring houses were nothing but dim, looming shapes. I couldn't see where the sound was coming from, but it kept up. It sounded like tanks were somewhere out there in the mist, roaming the streets, smashing into the houses.

I carried Mia down to the car, my jacket still wrapped around her, and got behind the wheel. My stomach started to growl as the first rays of the sun began to burn holes through the grey. I started the car and drove slowly down the street.

I drove for about a minute or so before I came across the source of the noise. It was a bulldozer, tearing down one of the houses. I stopped the car to watch. It drove into the front wall of the house, smashing its blade through a large picture window. Then it lowered the blade and tore apart the wall underneath the window. The bulldozer reversed across the muddy yard, then drove into another part of the wall a few feet over.

A flatbed truck and a couple of pickups were parked on the street. Men with white hard hats were drinking coffee from thermoses and watching the bulldozer work. I drove on when they all turned to look at me and Mia.

I kept on driving, past more half-built houses — or half-destroyed, I wasn't sure now — and then a long field bordered by a rusted chain-link fence and filled with bags of garbage. On the other side of the field were more houses, but there were cars in the driveways, and people walked up and down the streets.

I drove until I found a McDonald's. There was a car stalled in the drive-through line, so I parked in the lot and went inside. I ordered an Egg McMuffin and a coffee. When I came back out, Mia was awake and sitting up.

"Where are we?" she asked, looking around as I got into the car again.

"I don't know," I said. I cradled the coffee between my legs and started on the Egg McMuffin. The first bite burned my throat all the way down, but I didn't mind.

"Are you a friend of King's?" Mia asked. When I didn't say anything she began to scrape the dried mud from her face with her fingernails, then paused to look down at herself. "Where's my shirt?" she asked.

"It's a long story," I said.

"Did you do something to me while I was passed out?" She sounded more curious than upset. "You could have at least waited for me to wake up."

"I wouldn't touch you," I said.

"Yeah, right." She slid her arms into the sleeves of my jacket, did up the zipper.

"Not when you're in love with that dead guy," I went on.

"You don't know anything about it," she said.

"Oh, I know."

She lifted the Egg McMuffin from my hand, took a bite. "I saw this show on television the other day," she said. "This woman was in a car accident when she was pregnant. The dashboard was pushed into her stomach. The doctors couldn't hear a heartbeat. They told her the baby was dead and said they'd have to abort it."

I tried to take the Egg McMuffin back, but she held it away from me.

"Please," I said.

"But she wouldn't let them take it. She carried it through full-term, even though she thought it was dead. But when it came out, it was alive. She'd brought it back to life, just like that."

"Please," I said again.

"Now that's love."

"*Please.*"

WHAT HAPPENED TO OUR BABY?

THIS IS THE STORY of how I met Rachel.

I was working at one of the hospitals downtown at the time. They needed extras for training and disaster drills and the like. My job was to be a victim.

On my first day, a nurse made me get into a gown and lie on a bed in the hall — all the rooms were full, she said — and then the doctor in charge of the exercise came to see me. He was drinking coffee from a Starbucks mug.

"When the interns come, I want you to hold yourself here," he said, pointing to a spot on my stomach. "Make a lot of noise whenever anyone touches it."

"What's wrong with me?" I asked.

"Oh, it could be any number of things," he said.

"How about cancer?" I said. "Everybody gets cancer."

"If you like."

"What exactly are the symptoms?" I asked.

"It doesn't really matter," he said, watching a passing nurse and sipping from his mug.

"But how are they supposed to know what I'm dying from if I don't even know the symptoms?" I asked.

"This isn't that kind of exercise," he said. "You can't actually tell what's wrong with someone just by feeling their stomach."

"Then why are we doing this?" I asked.

"We're not testing them to see if they know what's wrong with you," he said, looking at his watch. "We're testing them to find out if they know the procedure."

I WORKED AT THE hospital once or twice a week. I was always suffering from some sort of deadly condition — brain tumors, strokes, heart attacks, that kind of thing. I researched them all in the library downtown so I could perform the symptoms properly. It was like I actually dying. I could have been.

I usually worked the same shifts as Rachel. She specialized in acting out mental disorders. She told me one day that I was one of the best patients she'd ever seen. We were lying in beds across from each other in a room on the children's ward, which was the only floor they had space on that day. "If they gave away Oscars for this business," she said, "you'd have my vote." She was chewing on something that made her mouth froth, and foam was running down her chin. She'd told me earlier that it had something to do with the condition she was supposed to have, but I thought it made her look rabid.

When the doctor brought the interns in, Rachel started to shake and shudder in her bed. She spat more foam out of her mouth and down onto her breasts, rolled her eyes back so I couldn't see anything but white.

The doctor stepped aside and waved in one of the interns, a young man with glasses and a goatee. He bent down beside Rachel and slipped his finger into her mouth. "Her airway seems to be clear," he said to the doctor, but that was all he managed because then he was swearing as Rachel bit his finger.

"That's why it's best to use pens to check airways," the doctor said as the intern clutched his hand to his chest. "Not the plastic ones, though. They can bite them in half, and then you get ink everywhere."

The next intern took a step toward the bed but then stopped as Rachel threw back her head and let out a long scream. It was so loud I actually had to cover my ears with my hands. The interns all looked at each other, but none of them stepped any closer. Then Rachel curled up into the fetal position and began to shake. She did that for a few seconds, then unrolled her eyes and winked at me.

How could I not fall in love with her?

SOMETIMES I DID my research at the hospital. I went around the wards and watched patients in their rooms or in the hallways, wherever I could find someone who had a condition I wanted to learn about. I was in there at all hours of the day, but the nurses didn't seem to mind. It was like I was a real patient. Some of them even commented on my acting.

"You're not dragging your legs enough," one of them told me when I was practicing my MS walk with some crutches I'd borrowed from a supply closet.

"Try taking off your clothes," another one said when I was sitting in the waiting room, working on my Alzheimer's look. "They like to take off their clothes when there are nurses around."

Even some of the patients gave me advice. A man who'd lost his legs in some sort of industrial press accident taught me how to use a wheelchair like I'd been in it for years. We spent the entire night racing up and down one of the halls, until I crushed the air hose of a woman on oxygen who'd come out of her room to complain about the noise. The nurses wouldn't let me back onto that floor for a week, and when I came back, the man in the wheelchair was gone.

Once, the nurses left a dead man on a bed in the intensive care hallway because they were too busy to take him down to the morgue. Someone was having a heart attack or something like that in the room at the end of the hall, so they were all in there. I lay down on an empty bed across from the dead man and studied him for a while, then tried to make myself look like him. He'd been left with his eyes open, so I stared at the ceiling for as long as I could without blinking, tried not to move at all. I only breathed when I absolutely had to. I could actually feel my heartbeat slow down. I wondered if this was what meditation was like.

One of the nurses came out of the room at the end of the hall and rolled the dead man and his bed into the elevator. I stayed where I was, not moving. A few minutes later, another nurse came out of the room and started pushing my bed toward the elevator. She screamed and jumped away from the bed when I sat up.

"Did I have you fooled?" I asked.

"I thought you were that dead guy," she said.

"Thank you," I said.

SOMETIMES, WHEN RACHEL and I were waiting for our shift to start, we'd get coffees from the cafeteria and wander around the hospital. We liked to make up stories about what was wrong with the people in the rooms we passed.

"Flesh-eating disease," I said of a man whose entire body was covered in bandages. "The nurses are afraid to touch him."

"Cancer," Rachel said when we went past a room with a woman on a lung machine. "But she never smoked a cigarette in her life."

"Attempted suicide," I said of a young woman who sat in a wheelchair by a window, drooling. "She took all the pills in her apartment when her boyfriend left."

"Self-inflicted gunshot," Rachel said of the same woman. "There was no boyfriend."

Rachel liked the intensive care ward the best. This is where they kept all the critically injured people, and we were only allowed in there during visiting hours. Most of the people in here were young, and many of them were dying from wounds they'd sustained in accidents and that sort of thing. They had a whole other wing for people who were dying of old age or disease.

"Imagine," Rachel said as we walked through here one day, "the lives of all these people are still going on."

I looked into a room at a man who appeared to be in a coma. He'd been asleep for as long as I'd worked at the hospital, and there were tubes going into both his arms. "I don't know about that," I said.

"I don't mean in here," Rachel said. "I mean outside. All these people have lives waiting for them out there. They have family, jobs, houses, cars, money, everything you can think of, just waiting for these people to get better and come back."

"But some of them aren't going to get better," I pointed out.

"Imagine if you could take their place," she said. "Just step into their lives and take over from them."

"I think there are laws against that sort of thing," I said.

"You could be anybody you wanted to be."

ON ONE OF OUR WALKS, Rachel and I found ourselves in the part of the hospital where they keep the babies. There was a room full of them on the other side of a glass wall, each one in its little incubator. Nurses wandered around the room, making sure they were all right. The babies closest to the glass waved their arms and feet at us.

"It's like we're their parents or something," Rachel said.

"But we're not," I pointed out.

"If it wasn't for the nurses, we could just probably take them and go, and they'd never know the difference."

"There are easier ways of getting children," I said.

"Are there?"

We watched as a nurse lifted one of the babies from its incubator and took it into a back room. There was a woman in a bathrobe sitting in a wheelchair back there, and before the door closed, we saw her hold out her arms for the baby.

"What do you think we'd be like if we were the parents of some of these kids?" Rachel asked.

"What do you mean?" I said.

She pointed at the nearest baby, a dark-haired thing with a face that looked as if it had been pushed down with sandpaper. "Who would we be if we were this kid's parents?"

I looked at the baby for a moment. "I'd be a lawyer," I finally said. "Corporate. You'd be ..."

"An accountant," she said. "We'd have a big condo downtown."

"And two cars," I said. "New ones."

"And a cottage on a lake somewhere," she said.

"And we'd vacation in the Caribbean every winter," I said.

She pointed out a baby that wouldn't stop crying. "What about that one?"

"With lungs like that," I said, "I'd have to be some sort of musician. Maybe even a rock star."

"I'd be your manager," she said. "We started out working together, and then we fell in love."

"On a tour of Europe," I said.

"We live in an estate outside the city," she said.

"I have gold albums and everything."

"We have maids and people who do our lawns."

"And more money than we can ever spend."

Rachel pointed to a baby at the back of the room. This one was tiny, half the size of the others, and it was in a different kind of incubator, one that was all enclosed in glass and had tubes running into it from machines. The nurses checked on this baby every few minutes, and they stopped smiling whenever they did.

"What about that one?" Rachel asked. "Who would we be if we were that baby's parents?"

"I'd be worried," I said.

I WAS ACTING OUT so many deadly diseases and conditions that I couldn't even tell when I was acting and when I was really sick. Once, I woke with what I thought was a real pain in my stomach. I'd been researching stomach cancer that week, and I knew all about the low survival rate, so I mentioned it to the doctor in charge of the training exercises when I went in that afternoon.

"I don't know," she said, "I was planning to test them on head injuries today."

"But I think this is a real pain," I said.

"Are you sure it isn't in your head?" she asked me.

When she brought the interns in, the first one shone a light in my eyes. "Are you feeling any pain or nausea?" he asked. The question was directed at me, but he was looking at the doctor.

"I have a pain in my stomach," I said.

"You mean your head," he said.

"No," I said, "it's in my stomach."

He looked at the doctor. "I thought we were doing head injuries today."

"But I'm not acting," I said. "I'm really in pain."

"I didn't study for abdominal pains," he went on. "This isn't fair." One of the other interns laughed.

The doctor checked her watch. "Let's move on," she suggested.

"But I think there's something really wrong with me," I said.

THE NEXT TIME we went back to the room with all the babies, the sick baby was still in its incubator with all the tubes hooked up to machines. It didn't look any bigger, and it didn't cry or wave its arms and legs like the other babies. It just lay there, looking up at the fluorescent lights overhead.

"Do you think it's going to live?" Rachel asked.

"I don't know," I said.

"Where are its parents?" Rachel asked, looking around. "What it needs are parents."

"Maybe they're sick too," I said. "Maybe they're in their own special incubators somewhere."

Rachel looked at me, then back at the baby.

"It'll grow if it thinks it has parents," she said. "It just needs to feel loved."

"Well, what can you do," I said.

"We'll be its parents," she said. She tapped on the glass. "Hello, baby," she said.

"What are you doing?" I asked.

"Wave to baby," she told me. She kept on tapping the glass, and the baby looked in our direction, as did one of the nurses.

"That's not our baby," I said.

"It doesn't know that," Rachel said. "It's still young enough that maybe it'll imprint on us."

"It's not a chicken," I said.

"Wave to baby," she said, "or it'll think you don't care."

I looked at the baby. It stared back at me, unmoving except for its shallow breaths. I lifted a hand and waved.

A FEW MONTHS after I started working as a victim, a pharmaceutical company hired Rachel and me for some drug trials. It took place in an old wing of the hospital that wasn't used any more. The hospital had sealed off the wing because it had been scheduled for demolition and rebuilding, but then the funds for the project had been cut off, and the wing had been left to collect dust, until they moved us in there.

There were maybe a dozen of us in total, all in one big room so the doctors could keep an eye on us. We lay in beds along the walls and watched a television they'd put in the middle of the room. All it played was commercials. Some of the others were normal people like me and Rachel, but some were actually sick. The guy in the bed beside me told me he was dying of cancer.

"Shouldn't you be in another ward then?" I asked him.

"They can't do anything about it," he said. "It's in my head. They'd have to cut out most of my brain to get at it. Then where would I be?"

"Is that a rhetorical question?" I asked.

"I'm hoping maybe these new drugs might do something," he said, but then he sighed and shook his head.

The trial ran for the weekend, and they gave us pills every four hours. They even woke us up if we were sleeping to make sure we took them. The pills all looked the same, tiny and blue, but the doctor in charge said that some of them were placebos.

"Please don't give me any of those," the man beside me said. "That's the last thing I need."

"I'll take his placebos if he doesn't want them," I said.

"That's not the way it works," the doctor said. "It's all random."

"Don't I know that," the man beside me said.

The water had been turned off in this part of the hospital, so we had to go back to one of the other wings if we wanted to use the washroom. One of the women in our group needed help walking there because the drugs she took made her fall down, and another guy lost control of his bowels in his bed, but I figured they were giving me placebos because there was nothing wrong with me.

But when I went to the washroom, I couldn't find my way back. I wandered the halls of the closed-down wing for what seemed like hours before I finally gave up. I lay down on the floor of one of the empty rooms and tried to go to sleep.

As soon as I closed my eyes, though, all the commercials that I'd watched on that television in the ward room started playing in my head. Only now Rachel and I were in them. We drove down a coastal highway in a gleaming new car, we met each other's eyes across a crowded bar and I slid a drink down the counter to her, we played one-on-one basketball against each other in a dark alleyway. I still don't know if it was all caused by the drugs or just a dream.

One of the security guards found me around dawn. He shone a flashlight in my eyes and kept it there even after I'd stood up. "We've been looking all over for you," he said. "We even checked the morgue downstairs."

"What would I be doing in the morgue?" I asked him.

"What are you doing here?" he asked, looking around the empty room.

When he took me back to the room where I was supposed to be, Rachel was just waking up.

"Where were you?" she asked me.

"I went to the washroom," I told her, climbing back into bed.

"I had this dream," she said, shaking her head. "We were living together."

"I want your drugs," I said.

RACHEL AND I STARTED checking on our baby whenever we were in the hospital. We'd stand on the other side of the glass and wave and smile and make faces. Once, Rachel even bought a silver helium balloon from the hospital's gift shop. It said Get Well Soon on one side, and the nurses tied it to one of the incubator's hoses. The baby waved its arms.

"Look," Rachel said. "It's like baby's trying to reach it."

"It's getting better," I said. I put my arm around her.

She didn't take her eyes off the baby. "It really is," she said.

Our baby grew stronger with each passing day. Soon it was waving its arms and legs together, and once I thought it even smiled at us, although Rachel thought it was just gas.

"I think it's going to live," I told her one day.

"But what kind of life is it going to have?" she asked. "That's the question."

"It's going to be an athlete," I said. "It's going to overcome all the odds and go on to become one of those success stories you see on television."

"I'll be happy as long as it's not in a wheelchair or anything like that for the rest of its life," she said. "I couldn't stand it if it was crippled."

"Even then, it'd still be a hero," I said. "Like that guy who rode his wheelchair all around the world."

"Imagine that," Rachel said, tapping her fingers on the glass. "Our baby, a hero."

BUT ONE DAY we showed up and our baby was gone. The special incubator was empty, and now the nurses didn't even look at it. The helium balloon was still attached to the hose, but it hung half-deflated in the air.

"Oh no," Rachel said, putting her hands over her mouth. "What's happened?"

"Hey," I said, pounding on the glass to get the nurses' attention. "What have you done?"

All the other babies started to cry at the noise, and one of the nurses waved at me to stop.

"Oh oh oh," Rachel said, staring at the empty incubator.

"It's okay," I said. "Don't worry, it's all right." I didn't know what else to do, so I pounded on the glass some more.

One of the nurses came through the door that led into the room. "Who do you think you are," she said, "upsetting the babies like that?"

"What happened to it?" Rachel asked. She put her arms around me, and I held her. "Is it all right?"

"What happened to what?" the nurse asked.

"What happened to our baby?" I said.

THE LAST TIME I worked as a victim was when the hospital staged a disaster simulation. It took place in the parking lot of a mall, on a Sunday morning. There were twenty of us, all made up with different injuries by professional makeup crews. We sat on the asphalt while they painted wounds on us. I asked for a bullet in the chest, but the woman who worked on me said it wasn't that kind of disaster. "It's an explosion of some sort," she said. "With toxic gas and all that." She did something to my head that made it look all burned and black, then ripped the top of my shirt open.

"Am I getting reimbursed for that?" I asked.

"Do you think you can vomit?" she asked, rubbing fake blood into my chest. Her hands were warm and strong, like a masseuse's. "We don't have any of the simulated vomit left, and they wanted everyone throwing up from the gas."

"What kind of gas is this anyway?" I asked.

"I don't know," she said. "All they said was gas."

"I don't think I can vomit," I said. "Maybe I should just take off my shirt and you can put blood all over me instead."

"I think we're about done here," she said. She turned to Rachel and worked on her for a while, giving her a slashed throat and covering one of her eyes with melted skin.

"How do I look?" Rachel asked me when the makeup woman was done.

"Perfect," I told her.

The hospital had hired a professional film director, a man by the name of Eden, to stage the event. He listed off all the films he'd worked on, but I'd never heard of any of them. He arranged us around a burned-out tanker truck they'd parked in one corner of the lot.

"This was in a real accident," he told us. "Two or three people got killed. So try to play off that, uh, realistic feeling."

Rachel put up her hand. "What do you mean, 'two or three'?" she asked.

"The fire department guys told me two bystanders died when it blew," Eden said, "but they never found the driver, so they're not sure what happened to him."

I looked at the cab of the truck. It was all melted, the metal fused together so tightly you couldn't see inside it. I wondered if the driver was still in there.

Eden spread us out around the truck and told us to lie down until the ambulances arrived. He walked among us, adjusting people's limbs and telling us to show more pain, that sort of thing. A couple of times he stopped and looked at the scene through a little lens hanging from his neck.

"All right," he said, when he was done, "I'm going to call the ambulances now. Try to stay in character when they get here."

Beside me, Rachel lay back and looked up at the sky, practised her moaning.

Eden walked over to the snacks table and grabbed a gasoline container from underneath it. He took it over to the burned-out truck and poured gas all over the hood and the cab. Then he tossed the can aside and took a lighter from his pocket, lit the truck on fire.

Rachel stopped her moaning and looked up. "There's no gas left *in* the truck, is there?" she asked.

"Are there going to be fire trucks too?" I called out, but Eden shook his head.

"No, this is just for, uh, effect," he said. "I thought it would make things look more real."

"*He* thought?" Rachel said, watching the smoke from the fire rise up into the sky. "Does the hospital know about this?"

"So no one's going to put out the fire?" I asked.

Eden didn't answer, though, because he was talking into his cell phone now. "Everybody's in places here," he said. "We're ready for the take."

I looked around the parking lot. People were pulling into parking spots around our taped-in area and getting out of their cars, wandering into the mall. Some of them looked our way, but no one actually stopped.

Eden frowned as he put away his phone. "Attention, people," he shouted. "There's been a delay. It seems there's been a real disaster in a chemical plant on the other side of the city, and our ambulances got sent there by mistake. They thought it was the exercise." People around Rachel and me groaned, but Eden held up his hands. "I want you all to stay in position," he said. "They're going to come for us as soon as they realize the mistake."

We lay there for a while longer, until the sun was almost directly overhead. I began to sweat, but I stayed in place. The smoke from the fire drifted down over us, and everyone began to cough.

"What if they don't realize it's a mistake?" Rachel wondered after maybe half an hour of this. "What if they think that other disaster is really the exercise all along?"

"Well, they'd better figure it out soon," I said, "because my makeup is starting to melt."

Just then we heard the sirens. "Thank God," Eden said and turned in the direction of the mall entrance. But it wasn't ambulances that drove in, it was fire trucks.

"No no no," Eden said.

There were three fire trucks in total, two regular ones and one of those smaller kind that the paramedics drive. They wound their way through the parking lot, honking their horns at the people going in and out of the mall as they tried to find their way to us. They had to circle around us once before they discovered a path through the parked cars. They drove into the exercise area, the lead truck going through the tape as it did so.

"Hey," Eden shouted, running at the truck. "You're breaking the scene integrity."

The trucks stopped, and firemen in full gear climbed out. One of them pushed Eden out of the way and started shouting at a group of others who were unrolling a hose. He pointed at the truck, which was still burning, and they dragged the hose toward it.

"I thought this was an exercise for the ambulance staff," I said to Rachel.

She shrugged. "As long as we get paid," she said. She closed her eyes and started to moan again.

The firemen turned on the hose and began spraying the truck. "No!" Eden cried and put his hands in the air. And now other firemen were kneeling beside the closest victims, looking at their fake wounds and reaching into their first aid kits.

"I don't think these guys know this is an exercise," I said.

Rachel opened her eyes and watched the firemen for a moment. Another group had unrolled a second hose and they began spraying water on the victims closest to the truck. The makeup melted away under the water, and Eden screamed and threw himself in the way.

"Someone else must have called them," Rachel said.

"So should we be playing our parts or not?" I wondered.

"We'd better ask Eden," Rachel said.

"Do you really think we should break the scene?" I asked.

But she was already on her feet and walking over to Eden, so I got up and followed her.

Eden was on his knees when we reached him, staring at the firemen as they started loading people onto stretchers. He held his hands clasped to his chest, like he was praying. There were more sirens in the distance now.

"What should we do?" I asked him.

"Are we still getting paid for this?" Rachel asked at the same time.

"Hospital," Eden said, only it came out more like a gasp.

"What about it?" I asked.

"Take me," he said, making that same gasping noise.

It was only then I realized that he wasn't praying, he was holding his chest. "I think he's having a heart attack," I said to Rachel.

Eden nodded and caught my hand with one of his. "Hospital," he said again. "Take me."

"I don't think so," I said, trying to push his hand off mine. "They'll take care of you here."

"Help," Rachel called, waving her arms at the firemen. "We need some help here." But none of them looked at us, because they were all busy with the other victims.

"Please," Eden said, squeezing my hand just a little.

"We're victims, not ..." I didn't know how to finish.

"I'll pay you," Eden gasped.

WE DRAGGED EDEN through the parking lot, to my car. "How much exactly are we getting paid for this?" I wanted to know as we drove around, looking for an exit.

"Hundred bucks," Eden gasped.

"Each?" I asked.

He shook his head. "Only have hundred," he managed.

"A hundred bucks to save your life?" I shook my head.

"And we're still getting paid for the exercise, too, right?" Rachel asked.

Eden didn't answer, just turned his head and looked out the window at the last bit of smoke rising from the truck. "Would have been perfect," he sighed.

We found the way out and went down the street in the direction of the hospital. More fire trucks drove past us, and I could hear sirens in all directions.

"This is really not a professionally run operation," Rachel said.

"Maybe we should start a union or something," I said.

"Maybe we should look for another job," she said.

"What would we do?" I asked.

"Something with benefits," she said. "In case we ever really get sick."

When we turned into the hospital entrance, I started to head for the parking lot, but Eden stopped me.

"Hey," he moaned from the back seat. "Emergency!"

"But I can't park in Emergency," I said. "It's just for ambulances and stuff."

"Emergency," Eden said again.

"I think you can park long enough to bring someone inside," Rachel said. "You just can't leave it there."

"All right," I said, "but I better not get towed."

None of that mattered, though, because as I drove into the Emergency area, I collided head-on with an ambulance coming the other way.

In the second before we hit, the ambulance driver and I stared at each other through our windshields. He opened his mouth to say something. Rachel screamed. Then the steering wheel came up and hit me in the face, and I couldn't open my eyes for a while.

When I finally managed to force them open once more, I saw Eden staggering through the Emergency doors. In the ambulance, the driver was slumped back in his seat, unconscious or dead, I couldn't tell. The other paramedic was standing in the rear of the ambulance, holding his head with one hand and the inside wall of the ambulance with the other.

"We'd better get out of here," I said, but when I looked over at Rachel, I saw that she was injured too. She was slumped back in her seat, and the windshield was cracked from where her head had hit it.

"Help!" I called out. I tried to undo my seat belt, but it was stuck. "Help!" I called again, this time to the paramedic who was conscious. He was out of the ambulance and stumbling around to the front of the vehicle now. He looked my way, then opened the driver's side door of the ambulance and dragged out the other paramedic. I pounded on the horn, but he didn't look back as he carried the other man through the Emergency doors.

I looked at Rachel again. I couldn't even see if she was still breathing or not. "Don't worry," I said. "I won't let you go." I leaned across as best I could with the seat belt holding me back, and I pinched her nostrils shut, blew air into her mouth. "I'll keep you alive until someone can save you," I told her. I kept it up until the nurses came out and took her away from me.

That was the first time we kissed.

JESUS CURED MY HERPES

AFTER I GOT KICKED OUT of The Code, I started driving out to the airport at night to watch the planes take off. I'd find an empty side street and sit on the hood of my car for hours. Sometimes the planes passed right over me, so low I could almost touch them. You could watch them for several minutes before they disappeared into the clouds overhead. There were always clouds over the airport.

There were other people out there who watched the planes, too. Most just parked on the street like me, but there was one group of men that met in front of a twenty-four hour garage. They were always there whenever I drove past, no matter what time of night. Five or six of them sitting in a circle of lawn chairs at the edge of the garage's parking lot, staring up at the sky and drinking beer from cans.

Once, I parked behind their row of trucks and wandered over to the edge of their circle. "Mind if I join you?" I asked. They all looked at me for a moment and then made noises like this was okay with them. One of them reached into a cooler at his feet and pulled out a beer, tossed it to me.

They didn't say anything at all as they waited for the next plane to pass, just kept staring up at the empty sky. I looked over at the garage. The doors were open, and inside I could see two men in grease-stained overalls bent over the engine of a car. One man would touch a part of the engine and shake his head, then the other man would do the same with another part of the engine. In the doorway of the garage, a woman was talking on a cell phone. "You don't understand," I heard her say, "I'm stuck here. I can't go anywhere."

A plane passed a couple of hundred feet over us just then. Over the noise of its engines, the man beside me shouted, "DC-10. Series 10. General Electric CF6-6 engines. 40,000 pounds takeoff thrust. Two hundred and fifty passengers, three cockpit crew. First flight made in 1970." The other men nodded and lifted their beer cans to their lips. Nobody said anything else until the next plane came. Then the man next to the first one who had spoken said, "737. 800 model. General Electric CFM56-7B engines. 27,300 pounds thrust. 189 passengers. First launched in 1965." They all nodded again and drank some more.

One of the mechanics got behind the wheel of the car and tried to start it up. The engine turned over and over but didn't catch. The other mechanic looked at the woman and shook his head. "I don't even know where I am," she shouted into her phone.

The men went around the circle until it was my turn. When the next plane passed overhead, they all looked at me. I looked up at the plane. "United Airlines," I said. "Probably going to New York." They kept staring at me until the next plane came, but even then they didn't say anything. They didn't speak again the whole time I was there, and they didn't offer me another beer after I finished the first one.

In the garage, one of the mechanics closed the hood of the car.

The other one went over to a coffeemaker in the corner and poured himself a cup. The woman put her cell phone in her purse and looked up and down the street. Then she went over to the car and sat behind the wheel, started turning over the engine herself. It made a slow grinding noise, like the engine was tearing itself apart underneath the hood. I could hear it all the way back to my car.

AND ONCE I SAW a plane struck by lightning. It was only a hundred feet or so off the ground when the lightning hit it, so quickly that all I really saw was the afterimage. There were two bolts — one came down from the clouds, while the other rose up from the wet ground — and they met somewhere in the fuselage. I couldn't see anything but white for a moment because of the lightning, but I felt the vibration from the thunder where I sat on the car.

I waited for the plane to fall from the sky but it didn't. Instead, it kept on rising into the sky, until it disappeared in the clouds. It was as if the lightning had never happened, or I had imagined it. For a moment I thought that perhaps everyone on board was dead, that the lightning had electrocuted them all in their seats, and that the plane was flying on its own now. I had a vision of it continuing to rise up into the sky, perhaps all the way out of the atmosphere and into orbit, everyone inside melted into their seats.

When I went home later that night, I turned on the television and watched for any stories about the plane. There was nothing, though, just a few brief sound bites about the salvage operation of a different plane that had gone down in the ocean a few days earlier. Nothing at all about any planes being struck by lightning. It was as if I were the only person in the world who even knew it had happened.

ANOTHER TIME I STOPPED at a twenty-four-hour coffee shop by the airport. It was surrounded by overgrown grass fields, and empty coffee cups and plastic bags filled the ditches at the side of the road. There was a tractor trailer with a cargo of live cows in the parking lot. A couple of them turned their heads to look at me through the slats of the trailer as I went inside, but the others just kept on staring at each other.

The driver of the truck was inside, looking at a road map spread out across the counter. He was following lines on it with a yellowed finger and shaking his head. "I just have no idea how I got here," he kept saying to the woman behind the counter, who wasn't paying him any attention at all.

I sat down with a coffee by the window, where I could still see the lights of the planes taking off from one of the runways. Every now and then one of the cows outside made a long, low noise, like the sound of a car horn slowed down. The truck driver pushed his hat around on his head each time he heard the noise, but he didn't look up from the map.

After a while, two women and a man all wearing the same kind of T-shirt came in. The T-shirt was black with the word BLESSING in red across their breasts. I watched their reflections in the glass as they went up to the counter.

"Last night I started shaking all over in bed," one of the women was saying. "It went on for ten minutes. I know because I was looking right at the clock the whole time. But I couldn't stop it."

"I had that electrical feeling myself," the other woman said. "You know, all the hair on my body was standing on end."

"It was like someone else had taken me over."

"It actually gave my cat a shock when he came over to see what was going on. He ran into the other room and wouldn't come near me all day today."

"I never felt a thing," the man said. "Haven't for a long time." He was going bald, and the whole time they were in there he kept pushing the hair he had over the bald spot.

"Stanley tried to climb on top of me during the middle of it," the first woman said, shaking her head. "He pretended he was in a rapture and couldn't control himself."

"That man," the other woman laughed.

The first woman bought an eclair and bit off one end, began sucking the cream out from inside. "But don't you worry," she said through a mouthful of cream, "I put a stop to that soon enough."

"I'd like to feel it again," the man said, frowning into his coffee. "Just one more time."

Both women laid their hands on him. "Maybe tonight."

"Yes, maybe tonight."

"Maybe," the man said, but he kept on staring into his coffee.

"Jesus Christ," the truck driver said, slamming his hand down on the map. "This doesn't make any sense at all." He stared out at his truck and sighed.

The people in the T-shirts looked away from him and didn't say anything else until they were on their way out. One of the women stopped at my table and bent over me. "I saw you watching us," she said.

"I wasn't," I told her.

"Would you like to talk about God?" she asked me.

"I don't think so," I said.

"Well, would you like to see him then?"

I WENT OUT with them to their car. The cows were pushing against each other in the back of the truck now, rocking the trailer from side to side. The woman who'd spoken to me said, "They feel it too."

"Feel what?" I asked.

"You'll see," she said, and for some reason the others laughed.

I left my car in the lot and got in the back of theirs, along with the man, who introduced himself as Hank. The woman who'd talked to me first said her name was Helen. The other woman, the driver, never introduced herself at all.

We went about a mile or so down the street, to a building that looked as if it had once been a warehouse, or maybe a factory. The parking lot was already full of cars, and the front doors of the place were wide open, lighting up a crowd of people standing outside. "Looks like the non-believers are out again tonight," Hank said.

"Atheists?" I asked, looking at the crowd. They held signs in their hands and were shouting at everyone that went inside.

"Oh no, they're Christians," he said.

"I thought you were the Christians."

"We are," he said.

"I don't understand," I told him.

"They're just jealous," Helen said from the front seat. "The Lord doesn't touch them like he touches us."

"I'm not so sure about this," I told them, but I got out of the car and followed them to the building anyway.

The people outside all wore the same kind of T-shirt, too, but this one was white with a red cross on the front. Other than that, these people didn't look any different from the people I was with. Their signs said things like JESUS DIED FOR YOUR SINS, NOT YOUR SEX and GOD DOESN'T BARK. "Satan!" they shouted at us as we approached. "Satan! Satan! Satan!" And one of them, a woman who looked a little like my dead grandmother, sprayed me with a Windex bottle.

"Hey hey hey," I said, but Hank took me by the arm and guided me through the doors. "Don't worry about it," he said. "It's only holy water."

"Do that again and I'll press charges," I shouted back at her over my shoulder.

The inside of the building was a large room filled with folding metal chairs. They were spread out in loose rows, with plenty of room between the rows and with a large aisle running down the middle of the room. The aisle ended in a large open area on the other side of the room, over which a giant wooden crucifix and carved Christ hung from the wall. Christ's body was all contorted, like he was having a seizure, and he looked like he was laughing or screaming, I couldn't tell which.

We sat at the back of the room, because most of the seats were already taken. There were other people wearing the BLESSING T-shirt here, but most were dressed in normal clothes or what I imagined passed for normal clothes with this crowd. Everyone was smiling and talking to the people around them. It looked like the sort of religious rally you see on television, but I'd always thought those things were staged.

"Good turnout," said the woman whose name I still didn't know. "God must have called a lot of people."

"It's going to be a special night," Helen said, nodding her head.

Hank didn't say anything at all, just stared at the Christ hanging over the stage.

After some time, a couple of the men in the audience got up and closed the doors. I heard one last "Satan!" from outside. Everyone seemed to stop talking and look at the Christ at the same time.

I could hear my own breathing, my heartbeat in my ears. Then the women around me began murmuring softly, too low for me to catch the words. Soon everyone in the crowd seemed to be talking softly to themselves, even Hank — everyone but me, that is. I kept waiting for something else to happen. I was getting hungry.

Then a woman stood up in the middle of the room, knocking her chair to the ground. "Jesus cured my herpes!" she shrieked. She pushed her way to the end of her row and ran down the aisle. Once she was underneath the Christ on the wall, she fell to the ground and started rolling around on the carpet, still shrieking the same words over and over. "Jesus cured my herpes! Jesus cured my herpes!"

I looked around the room, but nobody else seemed to be paying much attention to this. A pair of older ladies near me were even smiling and nodding at the woman rolling around on the ground.

A man in a suit near the front stood up and shouted, "Jesus turned my cavities into gold teeth!" He fell to his knees and started kissing the carpet. There were murmurs of "Hallelujah" and "Amen" from the crowd. A few rows in front of us, another man, this one in a post-office uniform, stood up and started weeping loudly.

"I think I'm going to leave," I said, but Hank put his hand on my leg. "Not yet," he said. "Not until you feel it."

"Feel what?" I asked.

"Just wait," he said. He didn't take his hand off my leg.

The murmuring in the crowd grew louder, and now I could hear some of what the people around me were saying. "Please, God, take me," a woman sitting directly in front of me whispered. "Just one more year," a man a few chairs down said. "Make it stop eating me," someone behind me said.

Then, as if on cue, a dozen or so people scattered around the room all stood up at once and began shrieking gibberish at the people around them. They acted as if they were saying things that made sense, but I couldn't understand a word of it. The entire front row of people fell to the floor and started convulsing there, as if they were all having simultaneous fits.

I watched it spread through the crowd, like some sort of virus. People ran hollering to the front of the room, where they fell to the ground and barked like dogs. Others writhed up and down the aisle like snakes. A man tore open his shirt, and the woman sitting beside him began kissing his breast, pecking at it like a bird. The air filled with screams and cries and hysterical laughter.

Beside me, Helen began laughing and fell to the floor. She caught hold of one of my pant legs with a hand and tried to pull me down after her, but I hung on to the chair. A few seconds later, Hank slowly slid off his chair, then started shaking and convulsing on the ground. His hand was still on my other leg, stroking up and down it. I kept pushing it away, but he kept putting it back. All around us, people were falling to the floor, touching each other all over, screaming hysterically.

Then the woman whose name I didn't know laid her hands on either side of my head and kissed me on the lips. I could taste the cream from the eclair, could smell her perfume. I went to push her away, but it was too late. It was as if someone else had taken control of my body.

I fell to the floor and felt myself shaking, flopping around like I'd been Tazered. My hands were everywhere on Helen and Hank's bodies, their hands everywhere on mine. The woman whose name I didn't know crowed like a rooster. I tried to scream but could only manage a long sigh. My whole body was burning.

Later, when I was away from that place and back in my car, I passed off what happened there as some sort of crowd hysteria. I'd read about that sort of thing before, how a few people in a crowd could cause everyone else to act the same way. It wasn't God, I decided, but some sort of psychological thing. Or maybe some sort of chemical pumped in through the air vents. Whichever. The important thing was it didn't last.

At some point during the night — it could have been hours or minutes after I fell to the floor, I couldn't tell — the protestors from outside opened the doors and ran in. They started spraying the people closest to the doors with their Windex bottles, all the while shouting, "Get thee hence, Satan!" and "In the name of God I evict thee!"

None of the holy water actually reached me, but once the doors to outside were open, I suddenly had control of my body again.

I got up and ran for the doors. Hank reached after me, howling, but I kicked him away. A protestor waved a sign at me — something about one of the passages in Luke — and I pushed her to the ground, stumbled outside.

It was raining out now, but I didn't care. I kept running, through the parking lot and down the road, back to the coffee shop. Once a car came from the direction of the church or whatever it was, and I hid in the grass at the side of the road, burying myself in the plastic bags there. For a while, I could still hear screams and laughter from behind me, even through the rain. My body was still burning from whatever it was that had happened in the church, but it faded a little more with the sound of each plane that passed overhead.

I never felt that way again in my life.

I SAW THE FIRST of the cows about fifty feet or so from the coffee shop. It was lying in the middle of the road, bellowing loudly. All four of its legs looked to be broken. It swung its head wildly at me, so I walked along the shoulder until I was past it.

There were two more in the coffee shop's parking lot. One lay just at the entrance to the drive-through. It was dead, its neck broken, head twisted around to lie along the top of its own spine. The other one was lying on the ground behind my car. There didn't seem to be anything wrong with it — it turned its head to look at me as I walked up — but it was blocking my way out of there.

The truck that had been carrying the cows was parked about a hundred feet away from the coffee shop. The back door of the trailer hung brokenly from its hinges, and I could see it was empty inside now. The cows were everywhere, more lying on the asphalt, others wandering up and down the road or grazing on the grass at the side.

The truck driver was standing by the rear of his truck and talking to the woman from the coffee shop as I walked up. "It's the damnedest thing I ever saw," he said, running his hand over the broken door. "They just started going crazy in there. For a moment, I thought they were going to tip the trailer. But then they busted out the back." He pushed his cap up and down on his head. "Bolt in the door must have rusted right through."

"Well, you can't just leave them here," the woman said. "It's bad for business."

"That's right," I said. "One of those cows is blocking my car."

We all watched one of the cows piss on the road for a moment, and then the woman said, "You'll have to round them up."

"And how am I supposed to do that?" the truck driver said. "Without getting trampled to death, that is."

"How'd you get them in the first time?" she asked.

"That's not my job," he said, shaking his head. "They've got special places for that."

"We could herd them with my car," I said, "if we can move the cow behind it."

They both looked at me for a moment, and then the truck driver said, "No, there's a very definite policy for moments like this." He went up to the cab of the truck and came back with a rifle. "How'd you like to make fifty bucks?" he asked me.

"That all depends," I said.

He waited until a plane was passing overhead, then shot the cow that had pissed on the road. It fell to the ground without making a noise and shook there for a moment. Several of the grazing cows looked over their shoulders at us and then moved a few feet deeper into the grass. For some reason, steam was rising from their hides now.

"I'm going to need help dragging them back into the truck," he said, chambering another round. "I can't move them on my own."

"I don't know," I said.

"Make it a hundred then," he said. "But that's all I've got on me."

"I'm going back inside," the woman said. "I've got to make fresh coffee."

"I could sure use another coffee now," the truck driver said. Another plane passed over us, and he shot one of the cows lying on the road. This one had a single broken leg. It tried to get up as the driver approached but it couldn't stand. Its eyes rolled wildly as he put the gun against its head and pulled the trigger.

He'd killed three more cows by the time the woman came out with coffee for each of us. "It's fresh," she said, "and on the house." She looked around at the dead cows and shook her head. "Given the circumstances and all."

We stood there for a moment, blowing steam from our coffee. Then the truck driver sighed. "I'm never going to make that deadline now."

He shot one of the grazing cows square in the head, but this one didn't go down. I saw bone chips fly off into the gravel at the side of the road, and blood sprayed as far as my shoes, but the cow just shook its head and stared at the truck driver.

"God's looking out for that one," the woman said.

The trucker lifted his cap off and then settled it back on his head. I saw that he was bald underneath. He fired another shot into the cow's head, and more blood and bone chips flew. The cow staggered this time but still didn't go down. It started running down the road. And now the surviving cows started after it, bellowing at us as they passed. Even the one that had been lying behind my car got up and went with them.

The truck driver aimed at the wounded cow once more, but this time his gun jammed. He worked at it for a moment, then swore and threw the gun to the ground. I was half expecting it to go off, but it never did.

"That was almost miraculous," the woman said. When the truck driver looked at her, she added, "For the cow, I mean."

"That wasn't anything but a jammed round," the driver said.

We watched the cows go down the road, leaving a trail of blood behind them. About two or three hundred feet down, they suddenly swerved into the field, heading towards the airport's lights. Even from this distance, we could see the cloud of steam rising from their hides.

"Well, if it wasn't a miracle," the woman said, "then I think it's as close as we're going to get."

WHERE WE LIVE

I WENT BACK to The Code a couple of months after I'd been kicked out. I was still out of work and almost out of money. It was the middle of the afternoon, and the place was almost empty. I was thinking about robbing it, but I couldn't see a waitress or bartender anywhere, although someone was laughing in the kitchen. I sat at the bar and dropped some of my last quarters into the electronic poker game there.

The only other person in The Code was Wyman. He was sitting at a table in the back corner, talking into his cell phone, but when he saw me he hung up and came over. He sat on the stool beside me, his eyes fixed on the television screen above the bar. There was a football game on, but I couldn't tell who was playing. "I don't have anything to sell you today," Wyman said. "I'm all cleaned out, and my supplier's gone out of town." This was Wyman's business: he sat at that table in the corner nine-to-five and sold drugs to the regulars and anyone else who could afford it. He used to work in the movie business as an extra or something, but I think he was making more money this way.

"That's all right," I said, "because I'm broke anyway."

He thought that over for a moment. "Well, you want to make some money then?"

"I just came in here to have a drink and play this game," I told him. But I'd already lost and I didn't have any more quarters.

Wyman nodded and lit a cigarette with a silver Zippo lighter. He kept flicking it open and shut while he watched the football game. "I need some help with a break and enter," he said.

I looked around the bar again, but I still couldn't see the waitress. I thought about going behind the counter to pour myself a beer. "I didn't know you were a burglar," I said.

He shook his head. "It's not like that. The stuff I'm taking is mine. But I have to break into the place to get it."

"I don't understand."

"It's my supplier's place." He leaned closer, glancing around the empty bar. "She's out of town, but all my stuff is there. I'm going to clean her out while she's gone."

"What's in this for me?" I asked.

"I'll give you two hundred dollars," he said.

"You want me to help rip off a dealer for two hundred dollars?" I laughed. "I don't know."

"You don't have to actually do anything," he said. "I just want somebody to go with me."

"I don't understand," I said.

"Call it moral support."

I looked at him closer. He hadn't shaved in days, and his upper lip was covered in little beads of sweat. "Who exactly is your dealer, Wyman?" I asked.

"My ex-wife," he said.

I stared at him. "You were married?"

WE WALKED DOWN the street to the coffee shop where Wyman had parked his minivan. Overhead, the clouds were racing past like the entire sky was some sort of time-lapse movie. There wasn't even a breeze down here.

The minivan's seats were covered with boxes and garbage bags full of clothing. Wyman had to pile them in the back to make room for me. "What's all this?" I asked, sorting through some shirts that couldn't ever have been in style.

"Jesse's been cleaning the apartment," he said, shaking his head. "She's making me get rid of all the clothes other women bought me. My closet's empty. It's like I'm eighteen all over again."

I looked at all the boxes and bags. "I've never had this many clothes in my life."

"I just can't bear to give them to Goodwill or someplace like that," he went on. "I mean, can you imagine some fucking stranger wearing my clothes?"

We drove to a subdivision in the north end of the city, a quiet and clean place that looked as if it had been abandoned and sterilized at daybreak. All the lawns were yellow. Wyman parked in front of one of the houses, in an empty driveway with dead grass sticking up through the cracks. There wasn't a single person in sight. I waited for Wyman to tell me what to do, but he didn't say anything or get out. He just kept turning in his seat to look at the other houses surrounding us.

"I've never done anything like this before," he finally said, turning off the minivan's engine and lighting a cigarette.

"Me neither," I said. "But this was your idea, remember?"

We sat there a moment longer, the clouds still racing past overhead, and then Wyman said, "All right then." We got out and went to the back of the van. Wyman emptied out a couple of the boxes, tossing the clothes over the back seat, and handed them to me. "Here," he said. "Take these to the side door."

"How big of a stash does she have?" I asked, looking into the empty boxes. They were bleach boxes, at least two feet deep and reinforced with extra glue.

Wyman crawled into the back of the van for more boxes. "What are you talking about?" he asked.

I went around the side of the house, to an old wooden door with a stained glass window. A mat on the step actually had the word Welcome painted on it, but you had to look close to see it under the dirt. All the blinds were drawn in the windows of the neighbouring house, so I figured no one was home there. I put one of the boxes over my fist and was drawing it back to punch through the stained glass when Wyman walked around the corner.

"What are you doing?" he asked.

"I thought we were breaking into the place," I said.

"Not like that," he said. He dropped the boxes he was carrying and took a gold card out of his wallet. I stepped aside as he inserted it between the door and frame. There was a soft click, and then he pushed the door open.

I looked around one more time before entering the house. In one of the neighbour's windows, a black-and-white cat had crawled in between the blinds and the glass. It sat on the windowsill, watching us with unblinking blue eyes. We went inside.

We were in a kitchen that was all wooden counters and shiny steel pots hanging from the walls. A skylight ran its entire length, giving the room a white glow. I could hear a clock ticking somewhere.

"Looks expensive," I said.

"Take off your shoes," he said, bending down to untie his own. "I don't want to be leaving dirt and shit all over the place. That's how they always track people down in the cop shows."

I kicked off my shoes. "What about hair fibers and that sort of thing?" I asked.

"They only do that for murders. As long as we don't kill anyone, we'll be fine."

I followed Wyman down the hall, into the living room. There was an Ikea couch and chair, a big-screen Sony television, a Toshiba stereo system, and some wooden bookshelves holding nothing but videotapes and CDs. The walls were covered with framed photographs, but when I looked closer, I saw the photos were the ones that had come with the frames.

"Where is she anyway?" I asked.

"Who?" Wyman said. He put the empty boxes on top of the Sony and started looking through the bookshelves.

"Your ex-wife."

"She's not here," he said. He began pulling videotapes off a bookshelf and dropping them into the boxes.

"I can see that," I said. I went over and looked at the tapes he was collecting. They bore handwritten labels such as Wedding Day and Disney World. "I thought we were here to steal some drugs," I said.

"You go right ahead," he said. "I'll be along in a minute."

I wasn't really sure where to look first, so I went upstairs. There were only three rooms up here: two bedrooms and a bathroom smelling faintly of bleach. I went through all the cupboards in the bathroom, but all I found was some toilet paper and tampons. The room was so clean I wasn't sure if it had ever been used.

The smaller bedroom was completely empty, nothing but vacuum cleaner marks on the carpet. I tried the master bedroom next. It was sparsely furnished, just a carefully made futon bed, a black dresser and two bedside tables holding chrome lamps with white shades. The walls were completely bare, something I'd never seen in a bedroom before. There were only a half-dozen dresses hanging in the closet, so I went through the dresser drawers. At first I was neat, gently pushing the clothes aside to look underneath them, and then I remembered this was a robbery. I dumped all the drawers out on the bed. I didn't find any drugs but I did find three hundred-dollar bills tucked inside a yellow sweater. I put them in my pocket and went back downstairs.

Wyman was sitting on the couch, pulling the insides out of a video tape. "What are you doing?" I asked him.

"I was going to record over them," he said, "but there's too many. We'd be here all day."

"I thought you were stealing them," I said, indicating the tapes in the boxes.

"Just the ones I'm in," he said.

I went into the kitchen and tossed the contents of the cupboards onto the floor, but I couldn't find drugs anywhere. I was thirsty by the time I was done, so I grabbed a Heineken from the fridge and wandered back into the living room. "I don't know," I said. "Maybe she knew you were coming or something."

Wyman was still ripping the insides out of the videos. He was covered in ribbons of the stuff now, and he'd somehow managed to cut one of his fingers, so little drops of blood were dropping onto the carpet.

I didn't know what to do, so I finished the beer in a couple of long swallows, then took the boxes he'd filled and went outside. There was a bit of a wind now, but other than that everything was the same. The cat was still in the window, watching. The day seemed like it would never end. I sat in the passenger seat of the van and put the boxes at my feet, then waited. I didn't want to go back into the house. It took Wyman nearly an hour to come out with the rest of the boxes. He opened the back of the van and shoved them in, tossing the loose clothes out on the lawn to make room.

When Wyman got back in, I asked him, "When do I get my money?"

He just looked at me for a moment, and then he started the minivan. We drove away from there slowly, the wind pushing his old clothes across the dried-out lawn behind us.

WHEN WE GOT TO Wyman's apartment, his girlfriend, Jesse, was stretched out on their leather couch, watching Letterman on the television. She was wearing a translucent silk nightgown and drinking something from a blue martini glass. The television was a big-screen Sony just like the one in Wyman's ex-wife's house. I decided not to say anything about that.

"What are you doing home already?" Jesse asked when we walked in, but Wyman didn't answer her. Instead, he walked through the living room and down the hall, disappearing into one of the bedrooms.

I put my box down in the entranceway and watched the television for a moment. "I didn't know Letterman was on in the afternoon," I said.

"It's a tape," Jesse said. She stood up and came over to look in my box. This close to her, I could see the little flowers she'd painted on her toenails and the Superman tattoo on her ankle. I'd asked her about the tattoo once, when we were dancing together at a warehouse party, but all she told me was that it had cost her an acting gig in a beer commercial. Wyman later told me she'd never auditioned for any beer commercial.

"What is this?" she asked, pulling out a tape with the label Honeymoon.

"I don't know," I said, but she wasn't listening to me now.

"No," she said. "These are not coming in here. Not where we live." She tossed the tape out onto the front walk and kicked the box after it. "You hear me, Wyman?" she called down the hall.

When he didn't come out of the bedroom, she asked me, "How could you let him do this?"

"I tried to stop him," I said in a low voice, "but I think there's something wrong with him."

"Jesus, there's no getting anything past you, is there?" she said. She started to laugh.

Wyman still hadn't come out of the bedroom. Outside, the wind had picked up, and now it looked like the clouds were falling right out of the sky on top of us.

"Wyman said he was going to give me some money," I told Jesse.

"No," she said, shaking her head. She pushed me out onto the step and kept repeating the word for the entire time it took her to close the door and lock it. "No no no no no no no no no no."

IT'S NOT MY RESPONSIBILITY

I WAS ON MY WAY to the liquor store when I passed him for the first time. An old man, fifty, maybe sixty, hard to tell exactly because his hair covered most of his face. He was lying asleep on the sidewalk outside the Happy Harbour, a bar where the lights were so dim it looked as if the people inside were underwater. He was right in front of the door, the way you sometimes see dogs outside a place, and drops of water from an air conditioner in a window overhead were falling onto his chest. He was wearing wool pants and two ski jackets, even though the day was so hot it felt like we were being sucked into the sun. And there was a little margarine container beside his hand, with some pieces of bread inside it.

The liquor store was at the end of the street. People lay in the passenger seats of the cars outside, eyes closed like they were unconscious. I spent the last of my money on two six-packs of the most expensive beer they had. Kennedy had called that afternoon to invite me to his wedding. He'd said that Rachel was going to be there. I thought she might call.

The man was still there when I came back from the liquor store, only now there was a woman with him. She was young, twenty or twenty-two, and she was wearing amber sunglasses and a Calvin Klein baseball cap. When I walked up, she was shaking him and saying, "Are you there? Are you there?" I tried to walk past, but she looked right at me. "I can't wake him up," she said.

I suddenly felt guilty, like it was my fault he was lying there, and I stopped. "He's probably just drunk," I told her. "I wouldn't worry about it."

"He shouldn't be sleeping in the sun," she said. She looked around and shook her head at the passing cars. "I can't believe people just let him lie here."

"I'm sure he's all right," I said. "Otherwise someone would have stopped by now."

When she brushed the hair out of his face, though, it was clear he hadn't been all right in some time. His face was a mask of broken blood vessels, and yellowish drool coated his chin. He looked as if he'd exploded inside. The woman stroked the side of his face, but he didn't even twitch an eyelid. "Who knows how long he's been lying here," the woman said. "With people just walking past."

"It looks like he's breathing regular," I said. "If he's breathing regular, then he's probably just sleeping."

She looked up at me and squinted a little through her sunglasses, like she was concentrating. Then she stared back down at him. "We should call someone," she said. "Paramedics or somebody like that. They'll take him to a shelter. Someplace cool, where he can sleep and not have to worry about exposure."

Her choice of words implied I was in this with her, so I put my beer down in the shade at the side of the building and squatted down on the other side of the man. I studied his chest for a moment. It didn't move much, but when it did, it was regular.

I thought about shaking him myself, but I didn't really want to touch him.

"We should call someone," the woman said again. When I looked at her, I saw her skin was all flushed and she was shaking a little. She kept biting her lower lip, like she was actually worried about this man.

I thought about Rachel calling, maybe right at this very moment. And then I thought about answering the phone and telling her how I'd saved the life of someone I didn't even know.

THE AIR INSIDE the Happy Harbour was cool and wet. There were five or six men sitting around a table in the middle of the room, with maybe two dozen beer bottles occupying the spaces between them. I didn't recognize any of the labels on the bottles. The men looked away from the television over the bar and at us as we entered, and their conversation drifted away, if there had been one in the first place. Then one of them, an old man with no front teeth, took off his John Deere cap and slapped the empty chair beside him with it. "Plenty of room here," he said. He was looking directly at the woman. The others didn't say anything, just looked at us with eyes that reminded me of dead fish.

We went over to the bar, where a Korean man wearing mirrored sunglasses was sitting on a stool, reading the paper.

"There's an unconscious man in front of your bar," I told him.

"Yeah, he's been there for about half an hour," he said. He didn't look up from the paper.

"And you just left him there?" the woman asked.

Now he stared at her. She looked into his glasses for a moment, then at me, then down at the floor. But that look had put me in charge.

"He wasn't drinking here," the Korean guy said. "It's not my ..." He searched for the word. "Responsibility."

"Maybe he just needs a kiss, darling," the man in the John Deere cap said. "Like Prince Charming." His laugh turned into a long series of coughs. No one else at the table made a sound. They stared at us like they were all mute. And they weren't all old either. There was a man in a UPS uniform who looked like he was around my age, and there was another man in shorts and a T-shirt who looked like he couldn't even have been legal drinking age yet. For some reason, he kept grinning at us.

"We need to call the police," I told the Korean guy. "Otherwise he could die or something. Because of the heat and all."

"He wasn't drinking here," the Korean guy said again and returned to the paper.

I looked at the woman. I was hoping that she'd tell me to forget it, that she'd walk outside and down the street without once looking back. We'd tried, at least. But she kept on staring at the floor.

We went over to the pay phone in the corner and I dropped in a quarter, dialed 911. We both watched the traffic outside as I waited for someone to pick up. A postman walked past the man outside without even glancing down at him. A woman answered after the third ring. "911," she said. She was laughing about something. "Do you need the police, ambulance or fire department?"

"I need somebody to take away an unconscious man," I said.

"One moment please." I waited through three more rings. A couple of the men at the table — the young guy and an old black guy who looked as if he'd been a weightlifter once but now seemed to be the victim of some sort of slow, flesh-eating disease — were still watching us. They were whispering back and forth and nodding at each other.

"Ambulance services," another woman said in my ear. "How can I help you?"

"There's an unconscious man on the sidewalk," I said. "I tried to wake him up, but he's out cold. He's been there for hours."

"How old is he?"

"Oh, he's old, maybe fifty or sixty."

The woman on the other end laughed. "You call that old?"

"What?"

"Never mind," she said. "Just give me the location."

I told her the address and then hung up. "Okay, help is on the way," I said. We went outside again and waited by the old man. The people driving past looked at us, looked at him lying there, but no one stopped.

After a while, the black man came out of the bar and stretched. I could hear his joints popping. Then he gently took hold of the old man's arms and dragged him a few feet to the side of the doorway, up against the wall of the neighbouring convenience store. "Gus doesn't want him on the property," he explained to us with a shy smile, before going back inside.

"He shouldn't have moved him," the woman said. "You're not supposed to move people when you don't know what's wrong with them."

"I think that's only for people with broken backs and stuff like that," I said. "I think this guy's problems are far different from that."

I heard sirens in the distance around the same time the young man came outside and lit a cigarette. Up close, I could see his white shirt had been washed so many times that it was now turning grey. He looked up and down the street, but his eyes kept coming back to the woman. I stood in between them, and he smiled, pulled a pair of sunglasses from his pocket and put them on. They looked like the kind of sunglasses you'd buy at a gas station.

"Here they come," the woman said needlessly when the ambulance came around the corner.

I started to lift my hand, but the young guy stepped in front of me and pointed to the old man with both arms, like one of those guys at the airport directing planes. The ambulance drove up onto the sidewalk beside us, almost hitting the woman. At the same time, a fire truck came around the corner from the other direction. Now the people driving past slowed their cars to watch us, and a few people standing at the traffic lights down the street began walking our way.

The paramedics came out of the ambulance fast but slowed down when they saw the old man. Both wore latex gloves and belt holsters carrying scissors. The one who opened the back doors of the ambulance had a grey beard even though his hair was brown. The other one walked in between us to kneel beside the old man. He was wearing knee pads the same colour as his uniform.

"He's been like this for half an hour," the woman told him.

"I tried to wake him up," the young guy said.

"No, *I* tried," I said, but the paramedic didn't pay attention to any of us. He held the old man's wrist loosely between his fingers, like he didn't want to touch him either, and looked at his watch for a while.

Gus came out and squinted at the fire truck as it pulled up in front of the bar. "There's no fire here," he said to me. "Why'd you call them?"

"I didn't call them," I said, but he just shook his head and went back inside, closing the door behind him.

Both paramedics were kneeling on the ground now, and the bearded one was shaking the old man by the shoulder. "I hate these calls," he said. I wasn't sure who he was talking to, though, because the first paramedic didn't pay him any attention either.

Two firemen climbed down off the fire truck and came over. They were wearing those fire-resistant pants and boots but no jackets, only T-shirts. All these people to help one man. I almost couldn't believe it.

"It's all right," I told them. "We've got it under control."

They glanced at me and then looked down at the old man. They didn't say anything.

"You live around here?" I heard the young guy ask the woman.

"He's probably just heat-stroked," I said to the watching crowd, which now numbered six or seven people. "He just needs to sleep it off."

The old man chose that moment to wake up. He half sat and looked around at all of us, then pulled the margarine container of bread to his chest with both hands.

"You see?" the bearded paramedic said to his partner, but I didn't know what that meant.

"How are you feeling?" the other one asked. The old man didn't answer. He kept staring at the gloves on their hands.

The bearded paramedic sighed and went over to the ambulance, closed its back doors.

"Aren't you taking him to the hospital?" I asked.

One of the firemen — a short, squat man with a sunburned face and a lazy eye — came over to me. "You the one that called this in?" he asked.

I glanced around. Everyone was watching me. "That's right," I said.

"And you couldn't wake him up?" The lazy eye drifted away from me, staring somewhere over my shoulder.

"Well, we tried."

"Well, he appears to be awake now." He walked back to the fire truck, his partner following along behind him. They climbed up into the cab but then didn't move, just sat there like they were waiting for another call.

The bearded paramedic had put on a pair of Ray-Bans now and was leaning against the side of the ambulance, his arms folded across his chest. His partner was still talking to the old man.

"You been drinking?"

The old man shook his head and smiled, then swiped one hand slowly over his face, the way a cat does when it cleans itself.

"You been taking any drugs? Methadone?"

The old man shook his head and smiled again, did the same thing with his hand.

"You got a place to stay? Relatives? Shelter?"

The old man took a piece of bread out of his container and nibbled it, looked around.

"You're going to take him somewhere, aren't you?" the woman asked the paramedic. "Where he can recover?"

The paramedic looked at her. "Recover from what?" he asked.

The old man pulled himself up the wall to his feet, hid the bread somewhere inside one of his jackets. He smiled even wider now. He seemed to be missing every second tooth.

The black man and the one wearing the John Deere cap had come outside sometime during all of this. They were still holding their beer bottles in their hands. "What's all the commotion?" the one in the cap demanded of the paramedics. "We have a police state now? Man can't even take a nap when he feels the need?"

"That's not what's going on here," I said, but he just waved his bottle in my direction and went on talking. "You cops," he said. "You just won't leave a man alone, will you?"

"Let's get out of here," the bearded paramedic said, and his partner finally nodded. He put on a pair of Ray-Bans himself, and the two of them got into the ambulance. I wondered if the city supplied their sunglasses, if it had some sort of contract with Ray-Ban, or if they had simply decided to buy matching pairs.

When I turned around again, the woman was gone, and the other members of the crowd were wandering off, back in the direction of the traffic lights. "Someone could have been dying somewhere," the black man said to me, and then he and the others

PLEASE 99

from the bar went back inside. It was just me and the old man now.

He watched the ambulance drive down the street and, when it turned the corner, he sat down again. He didn't look at me, just squinted up at the sun and yawned. Started humming and swaying a little.

I stepped around the side of the building to get my beer. It was gone. I looked over at the fire truck, but none of the firemen looked my way as it pulled into the traffic.

"Did you see who took my beer?" I asked the old man, but he just shook his head and closed his eyes.

I went inside the Happy Harbour. Everyone was sitting around the table again, and the man in the John Deere cap was telling some story about the time he'd gotten into the back of a police car because he thought it was a cab. He stopped when I walked in, though, and they all turned to look at me.

"Someone took my beer," I said.

"You didn't order a beer," Gus said from behind the counter.

"That's right," the man in the cap said. "You just came in to use the phone. Remember?"

"Someone took the beer I put down outside," I said. "Two six-packs. I put them down in the shade and someone walked off with them." I kept watching the young guy. He wouldn't stop smiling at me.

"I bet it was that drunk outside," the man in the cap said. "He probably needed a drink to get back to sleep."

"You try and help a man out," I said, "and this is the way society treats you."

"Take it somewhere else," Gus said from behind the bar.

"You should grow up," I told the young guy. "And you should do it fast."

His smile pulled back to show all his teeth, "What are you saying, man?" he asked. He got to his feet. "What are you saying?"

"Hey hey hey," Gus said. "You get out of here," he told me.

"Maybe I should call the cops," I said.

"You get out of here now," Gus told me, "or I'll call the cops on *you*."

HAPPILY EVER AFTER, I GUESS

THIS IS THE STORY of how Rachel and I got married.

After we moved in together, I had to look for a new job. The hospital had stopped calling us in after that accident in their Emergency area, and we were almost out of money.

I got up at eight in the morning every day and showered and dressed in my nicest clothes. I made myself a lunch and Rachel kissed me on the cheek as I went out the door. It was like I was really going to work.

I had a routine. I went to the variety store at the end of the street and bought a paper and a coffee. Then I went another block over, to a park between a dollar store and a row of houses with boarded-up windows. I sat on a bench and drank my coffee, looked over the classifieds. Rachel had given me her lucky pen to circle ads with, but there was never anything I was qualified for.

There was a fenced-off playground in one corner of the park. There were maybe a dozen children that played in there every day, and a pair of women who watched them. There were always another five or six people and their dogs in the opposite corner of the park. The people drank coffee and talked while the dogs fought.

And there was another man with a paper who sat on a bench near mine. He was there every day by the time I arrived. He wore a suit and read the entire paper, not just the classifieds. The first day I was there, he saved my life.

One of the dogs from the other end of the park — a large Rottweiler — came running over when I sat down on the bench. It stopped a few feet away from me and started growling. I looked at the people with the rest of the dogs, but they were still talking to each other and waving their coffee cups in the air. With each growl, the dog moved closer to me.

"It doesn't know you," the man in the suit called out to me. "It thinks you're a stranger."

"I am a stranger," I said, and the dog moved closer. It was almost touching me now.

"Just give it something so it knows you're friendly," the man said.

I didn't have anything but my lunch, a sandwich in plastic wrap. I dropped it to the ground. The Rottweiler gave me one last growl, then picked up the sandwich in its jaws and ran back to the other dogs.

"That was a close one," I said to the man in the suit, but he just nodded and turned to the business section of the paper. I watched the Rottweiler eat my lunch on the other side of the park, and then I watched the clouds shift back and forth overhead for a while. When I looked at my watch, it wasn't even ten yet. I wandered over to the playground and leaned on the fence there. The kids didn't notice me, but the two women watching them did. They stopped talking and kept glancing my way, as if I was going to run off with one of the kids if they stopped looking at me for even a moment.

It made me wonder how I would have turned out if I'd had somebody like that watching out for me.

DURING THIS TIME, Rachel began working for a chat line, the kind you see advertised on television after midnight. She told me about it when we were watching a movie in bed one night, and I asked her if it was one of those phone-sex jobs.

"Oh no, it's nothing like that," she said. "I'm just going to be talking to people."

I muted the television and sat up. "You're going to be talking to people?" I asked. "Or you're going to be talking to men?"

"Women don't really call these lines," she said. "That's why they're hiring me."

"But why do the men call?" I asked.

"Look," she said, taking the remote from my hand and turning the volume back up, "one of us has to work."

Rachel worked the night shift at the chat line. She took the bus to the call center, which was in this old hotel at the edge of downtown. The company she worked for had made some deal to rent an entire floor, and each of the operators had a separate room.

"It's like you're a prostitute or something," I said when she told me about it over breakfast after her first shift.

"It helps me get into character," she said. "I even have a name. Velma."

"What kind of name is that?" I asked.

"I think it's supposed to be Russian," she said. She spoke in a thick accent that didn't sound like anything I'd ever heard before. "Russians are in style these days."

"Is everyone there Russian?" I asked.

"No, we have a couple of Asians, a German, an Australian, even a Brazilian." She laughed. "But everyone playing them is white."

I went to the counter and poured myself a coffee, then went over to the kitchen window. It looked out onto the street, and for a while I watched people go past in buses or cars, on their way to or from work.

"What kind of calls do you get?" I asked.

"I had this one guy who wanted to talk about his mother," she said. "Then he asked all sorts of questions about mine."

I turned back to her. "What else did he ask about?"

"You don't want to know," she said, shaking her head and laughing.

"Yes, I do," I said.

"No, you don't."

AFTER I'D GONE to the park another few days, the man in the suit offered me a cigarette. I went over and took it, even though I don't smoke, and sat on the corner of his bench. The Rottweiler chased a Lab across the park to us, and for a moment both stopped to sniff at our ankles. I was ready to give them my sandwich, but they moved on without even growling at us.

"So what do you do?" I asked the man.

He watched the dogs a moment before answering. "I'm a broker," he said.

"Stocks?" I asked.

"Something like that," he said. He looked at me. "What about you?" he asked.

"I'm self-employed," I told him.

"All right then," he said, nodding.

We sat there in silence for a moment, him smoking and me pretending to smoke, and then I asked, "So how long have you been coming here for?"

He looked all around the park now, and for a moment he didn't answer. Then he said, "About a month."

"And she hasn't figured it out yet?"

"I have savings," he said. "I can probably go another month."

"And then what?" I asked.

"And then?" He blew smoke at the sky. "Then I guess it's over."

"I don't think I can go that long," I said.

"Oh, you'll be surprised what you're capable of," he said.

"What do you do when it rains?" I asked.

"I drive," he said.

"Drive where?"

"Nowhere."

We didn't say anything else until the cigarettes were finished, and then I said, "One of us should bring a chess set or something like that."

"Why would we want to do that?" he asked, looking back at me.

"You know, to pass the time," I said. "We could be like those people you see on television, the ones that play chess in parks all day long."

"But this isn't a permanent kind of thing," he said.

"But it could be," I said.

"I'm still working, in a way," he said. He patted the paper beside him. "I'm keeping up with the stocks. In case they call me back." When I didn't say anything, he added, "Or in case someone else calls me."

"Have you applied for any other jobs?" I asked.

"I'm doing lots of research," he said.

"Well, I still think we could play chess or something," I said.

He picked up the paper again. "I'm not one of those people," he said.

I got up and went over to the playground again. One of the women came over to where I leaned on the fence, but she was careful to stay out of arm's reach.

"Can I help you with something?" she asked.

"Are you looking for help?" I asked.

"What do you mean?" she said.

"I need a job," I told her. "And I'm good with kids."

"I'll get back to you on that," she said and walked back to join the other woman.

A boy of maybe five or six went down the slide. When he reached the bottom, he looked at me. I waved at him and he waved back.

"Don't talk to strangers," the woman who'd spoken to me told him.

"I'm not a stranger," I called over to her.

The boy stared at me until the woman came over to stand between us.

"Ask the dogs," I told her. "They know me."

"If you don't leave now," she said, "I'm calling the police."

RACHEL STARTED OFF SLOW at her new job, only two or three nights a week, but it wasn't long before she was up to five or six nights.

"People have been requesting me," she told me as she was getting ready for work one night. "They've been phoning the main line and asking for my home number."

"They're not going to be calling here, are they?" I asked.

"I'm just going to work more shifts," she said, putting on her coat. "We may even try some different personalities."

"Why would you do that?" I asked. "It sounds like enough men are calling you now."

"We want to get the ones that aren't calling," she said, kissing me on the cheek and walking out the door.

I barely saw her at all. I slept alone in the bed most nights, and when she came home, I got up to go look for work. Once, she came home and stood at the foot of the bed, watching me until I woke up.

"What are you doing?" I asked, sitting up and staring back at her.

"I was thinking about you last night when I was talking to this guy," she said, "and I forgot what you looked like."

After maybe two weeks of this, I asked her what kind of men were calling. I was taking a bath, and she was sitting on the edge of the tub. "Are they all unemployed?" I asked. "Are any of them calling from jail or anything like that?"

She put a hand in the water and moved it around but didn't touch me. "Most of them are businessmen," she said. "At least, that's what they tell me."

"What kind of businessmen?" I asked.

"Executives away from home on business," she said. "CEOs taking a break at the office. That sort of thing."

I stared at her but didn't say anything.

"These calls are expensive," she said, taking her hand out of the water and drying it on her pant leg. "Not everybody can afford to talk to me."

I STOPPED GOING to the park after the incident with the man in the minivan. The first time I met him, he cruised around the park twice, looking in at us, before he parked on the side of the street. He sat there for another few minutes before he finally turned the engine off and got out.

He walked right up to me and stood between me and the sun, so that when I looked up at him, I couldn't see his face.

"How'd you like to make a hundred bucks?" he asked.

"Who do I have to kill?" I said, but he didn't laugh.

We went back to his van. There was a baby seat sitting loose in the back, and a couple of brightly coloured plastic rings. The man in the suit watched as we drove away. I waved at him, but he just looked back at his paper.

"So what's this all about?" I asked the other man.

"I just need you to do something for me," he said. He kept checking all his mirrors, like he thought someone was following us. "It won't take long," he added.

He drove us a few streets over, to a postal station. He parked in the lot and looked all around one more time. Then he reached into his pocket and took out a driver's licence. "I want you to go inside and open a post-office box," he said. "They'll ask you for ID. Give them this." He handed me the licence.

I took it and looked at the photo. It was a man with a beard and glasses. I didn't look anything like him. Neither did the other man.

"This is some sort of fraud, right?" I asked him.

"They don't usually look at the card all that closely," he said. "If they do, just tell them you shaved the beard since you got your licence."

"What if they don't believe me?" I asked.

"Then run," he said. "But don't run back here."

I went inside and registered for the post-office box. The woman who filled out the forms and gave me the key didn't even look at the photo on the licence, just wrote down the number. I was back in the van in under ten minutes.

"Who is this guy anyway?" I asked, handing over the licence and the key. "Is he dead?"

"No, no, it's nothing like that," the other man said, looking around the parking lot. "I just borrowed it."

"Okay," I said. "Whatever. Where's my money?"

He took out his wallet, which was bulging with money, and paid me in twenties. It looked like there was a thousand dollars in there, and maybe a dozen credit cards.

"Jesus," I said. "I should just rob you here."

Now he laughed. "Where can I drop you off?" he said.

I CALLED THE CHAT LINE Rachel worked for. I bought a phone card at the convenience store down the street, so she wouldn't be able to track it to me. I turned off all the lights in the bedroom and muted the television, then called the number. When a woman whose voice I didn't recognize answered, I hung up. I called back until I got Rachel.

"Who's this?" she said when she came on the line.

"This is Jack," I said.

"Jack," she said, and I could tell from the tone of her voice that she was smiling. "This is Velma, Jack."

"Hello, Velma."

"Hello, Jack."

There was a creaking in the background, which I took to be the springs of the bed in the hotel room.

"So what do you do, Jack?" she asked.

"What do you mean?" I said.

"What kind of job do you have?"

I didn't say anything for a moment. Then I said, "I'm a broker."

THE MAN WITH THE VAN came back the day after I first worked for him. This time he waited in the van, its engine running. I went over and opened the door. "Have you got another job for me?" I asked.

He smiled but didn't say anything. I got in.

We drove across the city, to a discount mall. He parked in front of an appliance store and took a gold card from his pocket, handed it to me. I looked at the name. Veronica Young, it said.

"Here's a list of what I want," he said, giving me a slip of paper.

I took it but didn't look at it. "But this is a woman," I said, indicating the credit card.

"If they ask, say it's your wife," he said. "But they probably won't ask."

"What happens if I get caught doing this?" I asked. "Who exactly is breaking the law here, is it me or you?"

"If they call anybody, then run," he said. "But remember, don't run back to me."

I went into the store and looked at the list. A television. Laptop computer. CD player. There was a list of specs beside each one. I found a man who worked there in one of the aisles and gave him the list. "This is what I need," I said. "For my wife."

He helped me load up a cart with the boxes and I took it to the cash area. The woman who rang everything through didn't look at me or the card. I had to leave the cart in the store, so I carried everything just outside the door and waited for the man in the van to pick me up.

We loaded the boxes into the back of the van, beside the baby seat. "If you want me to keep doing this," I said, "you're going to have to pay me more."

He smiled at me again. "Just a couple of days on the job," he said, "and already you're asking for a raise."

I PAID RENT with the money that I made working during the days. When Rachel asked me where the money came from, I told her I had some money in savings. What I didn't spend on rent, I spent on phone cards so I could talk to her at night.

I liked to talk to her about my job. That is, I liked to talk to her about Jack's job. "I administer various funds," I told her when she asked what was involved in being a broker. "I make sure we're always getting the highest returns on our investments."

"That doesn't sound very exciting," she said.

"It's not," I said. "But with my salary, I can buy whatever I want."

"That sounds much better," she said.

"In fact, I'd like to buy you dinner some night," I said.

"But we barely know each other," she said.

"What better way," I said.

"Where would we go?" she asked.

"One of the places downtown," I said. "The kind where you can only get in if they know you."

"And do they know you?" she asked.

"They all know me," I said.

"What about dress codes and all that?" she said. "I don't really have anything fancy."

"I'll buy you a nice dress," I said. "Wherever you want."

"A designer boutique," she said. "I've always wanted to shop at one of those."

"Fine," I said. "Then we'll go out to dinner."

"Someplace with martinis," she said. "If you're in a fancy dress, you should be drinking martinis."

"All right," I said.

"And people doing drugs in the bathroom. The good kind."

"And we eat the most expensive meal they have," I said.

"What would that be?" she asked.

"Something from another country," I said. "Something endangered."

"And for dessert," she said, "something flaming."

"I pay for it all," I said, "and then I take you back to your place."

"You move quick, don't you?" she said.

"And I kiss you on the doorstep," I said.

"Fresh," she said.

"And then —" I said.

"And then I go inside," she said. "Alone."

"Really?" I asked.

"We have to leave something for the next date," she said.

I WORKED EVERY DAY for the man with the van. We bought things all over town with his credit cards, opened more post-office boxes, even went into banks and cleaned out people's accounts with their own bank cards. I was making more money working for him than any other job I'd ever had.

One day, as we drove away from a Wal-Mart with a load of vacuum cleaners, I asked him what his wife did.

"What do you mean?" he asked, staring into the rear-view mirror.

"Does she work? Does she stay at home with the kids?"

"What wife?" he asked. "What kids?"

"You don't have kids?" I asked.

"What makes you think that?" he said, looking at me now.

"The baby seat in the back," I said. "I thought ..."

He laughed and shook his head. "What makes you think this van is mine?" he asked.

ONE NIGHT, WHILE we were eating dinner and watching television before Rachel had to go to work, I asked her if she'd had any interesting calls lately.

"I have this broker who keeps calling me," she said, not taking her eyes off the television. "He asked me out on a date the other night."

"What did you tell him?" I asked.

"I told him no," she said.

"Really?" I said.

Now she turned to look at me. "Isn't that what I should have told him?" she asked me.

"Of course," I said.

She looked back at the television. "So," she said, "how's the job hunt going?"

"It's tough out there," I said. "No one's hiring." When she didn't say anything, I added, "I might have some interviews next week."

"That would be good," she said.

"Yes," I said. "It would."

I didn't say anything else for a moment. Then I said, "So tell me what this broker is like."

BUT I HAVEN'T TOLD YOU about the incident with the other man yet, the one that made me stop working for him.

He picked me up at the park one morning but then didn't take me anywhere. We just drove around the neighbourhood again and again. We went past where I lived twice, and I imagined Rachel inside, sleeping in the bed I had just left.

"You're not a cop, are you?" the man asked after we'd been doing this for maybe twenty minutes.

"After all we've been through," I said, "you could think that?"

"I had to ask," he said. We drove around in silence for a few minutes more. Then he asked, "So what do you charge, anyway?"

"What do you mean?" I asked.

"You know," he said. "When you're working."

"Do I actually hear what I think I'm hearing?" I asked.

"It's all right," he said. "I'm not a cop either."

"Where did you get the idea that I was ..." I didn't know what to say.

"Well, you were in that park," he said, looking at me. "I thought you were working."

"I wasn't working," I said, "I was looking for work."

"What's the difference?" he asked.

"Oh, there's a whole world of difference," I said.

"Anyway," he went on. "What do you charge?"

"That's not what I do," I said. "You couldn't pay me enough."

"No?" he asked.

"No," I said.

"What about if I gave you everything in my wallet," he said. "Would that be enough?"

THE NEXT TIME I called Velma, I asked her to marry me.

"This is a bit sudden," she said. "We haven't even met in person."

"I feel like I know you," I said.

"I don't think I'm ready for marriage," she said.

"I've even got a ring," I said.

"You've got a ring already?" she asked. "But I haven't even said yes yet."

"But you will," I said.
"How do you know?" she asked.
"Because this is my call," I said.
"What would we do if we were married?" she asked.
"I don't know," I said. "Happily ever after, I guess."
"Well, that doesn't sound so bad," she said.
"Why don't we meet somewhere?" I said. "In real life?"
"I'm not sure if I'm ready for that kind of commitment," she said.
"When's your next night off?" I asked.
"Tomorrow," she said.
"I'll meet you at the mall downtown," I said. "The south entrance. Six o'clock."
"How will you know what I look like?" she said.
"I'll know," I said.
"All right," she said. "Maybe."
"And don't tell your boyfriend about this," I said.
"Who said I had a boyfriend?"

I REALLY DID have a ring. I'd bought it from an old man in the street. He'd been trying to sell it for months. Every day he stood in front of the Starbucks by my place and offered the ring to anyone who walked past. He was there even when it rained, wearing a black wool overcoat and cap despite the fact that it was summer at the time. He never spoke, just held the ring out in his hand. It was a thick golden band with no markings on it. He looked as if he hadn't talked to anyone in years.

Once, an older woman started yelling at him. "How dare you," she said over and over. She was leaning on a walker herself. The man just stood there, holding the ring out to her. Together they blocked the entrance to the Starbucks. A crowd formed around them, waiting to get in. "What would your wife think?" the woman shouted at him. "What do you suppose she's thinking right now?"

I bought the ring from him a few days later. I went inside, bought a latte, then went back out and asked him how much he wanted for the ring. He still didn't speak, just shuffled a step closer to me. His brows went up and down, like he was signaling something to me in code.

I took a ten out of my wallet. "Is this enough?" I asked.

He took another step closer. Now I could smell his sweat. His mouth worked but still nothing came out.

I pressed the ten into his hand, took the ring out. "All right?" I asked. He kept shuffling toward me. I took out another ten and put it in his hand, along with the first. His hand clenched into a fist around the money.

I backed away from him, but he kept coming. All the way down the sidewalk he followed me, shuffling at the same pace, staring at the ring I held in my hand. I crossed at the corner just as the light changed, but still he came on, straight into the traffic. That was the last I saw of him, standing there in the middle of the street, amidst all those cars, hand still stretched after me.

AFTER I STOPPED GOING to the park, I spent a few days at the art gallery downtown. The first morning, I stood in line to see how much it would cost to get in. The woman behind the counter told me it was pay-what-you-can.

"What if I can't pay anything?" I asked. "Do I get in for free?" I still had some money from working for the man with the van, but I didn't know when I'd work again.

She adjusted her glasses before answering. "There are suggested minimums," she said. "Most people pay five dollars."

I put a dollar on the counter and she stared at it. "It's all I have," I said.

"All right then," she said, printing me a ticket.

"Really," I said.

The inside of the gallery was cool and dark. There was hardly anybody else in the place at this time of day. I wandered from room to room and looked at paintings I didn't understand.

After about an hour or so of this, I found myself in the medieval room. The walls were covered in wood carvings of people in churches, and there was a large Christ on a cross on one wall. I sat on a bench in front of the Christ. The room was completely silent. I couldn't hear anything but my own breathing. It was like the city outside of the gallery didn't exist at all.

I lay down on the bench and stared up at the Christ. It was made of some sort of painted wood, and it hung slightly off the wall, like it was about to fall on me. After a time, the overhead lights turned off and I was in the dark, except for a small spotlight in the ceiling that lit up the Christ's face. It kept on staring at me, until I closed my eyes.

I don't know how I long I slept. I was woken by a woman in an art gallery uniform. "There's no sleeping in here," she said. "You have to go somewhere else to do that."

"I wasn't sleeping," I said. I sat up and rubbed my eyes. The lights were back on now. "I was praying," I told her.

She backed away from me, putting a wooden altar covered by a glass case between us. "Don't make me call security," she said.

RACHEL TOLD ME she had to go to work the night I was supposed to meet Velma at the mall.

"I thought it was your night off," I said. "I thought maybe we'd do something."

"I got called in," she said. "We need the money."

"True," I said.

"Maybe someday you'll get a job too," she said.

"I'm sure," I said. "Any day now."

AFTER SHE LEFT, I drove downtown and parked in the mall's parking lot. I went into the coffee shop across the street from the south entrance and bought a coffee, then sat in a window seat. I watched for Velma. Six o'clock came and went. Then seven. At eight, I gave up. Velma never came.

I went home and phoned the chat line until I reached her. "What are you doing?" I said. "We had a date."

"You can't keep calling here," she said, and now her Russian accent was completely gone.

"What do you mean?" I asked. "The whole point is that I keep calling."

"I'm working," she said. "Do you understand that?"

"So it's over? Just like that?"

"I'm *working*."

WHEN I WENT BACK to the art gallery, I didn't go anywhere near the medieval section. Instead, I went to the modern art section. There was another man there, sitting on a bench and drinking a coffee while he looked at a life-sized picture of Elvis dressed in a cowboy outfit. Behind him, on the floor, was a pile of empty fast-food containers.

"Someone's left some garbage here," I said.

The man looked over his shoulder. "That's not garbage," he said. "That's an exhibit."

"What do you mean?" I asked.

"That's art," he said.

I looked down at the pile of containers. There were even little bits of food left in some of them. "Are you sure?" I asked. And there were other little bits of garbage mixed in with the containers: crumpled photographs, movie ticket stubs, a doll's head.

"They paid almost ten thousand dollars for it," he said.

"They paid ten thousand dollars for garbage?" I said.

"They paid ten thousand dollars for art," he said. When I just stared at him, he added, "It's an installation piece."

"I've never had that much money in my life," I said.

"Who has?" he said.

"How do you know all this stuff?" I asked him, sitting beside him on the bench. "Do you work here?"

He shook his head. "No, I'm more of a collector."

I looked at the picture of Elvis. Actually, there were four pictures of Elvis, side by side. He was in the same pose in each, pointing a gun at me, but the colours were progressively more washed out as the panels went along, until he was almost invisible in the last one.

"What do you think this one's worth?" I asked.

"That one's a Warhol," the man said. "It's priceless."

I stared at it. "I don't understand," I finally said.

He moved closer on the bench. "It's about commodification of the individual," he said. "See how Elvis is repeated so many times, until he becomes nothing more than a product?"

"Like those soup can paintings," I said.

"Exactly," the man said, nodding and smiling like he was my teacher.

I shook my head. "I could do this," I said.

"But you didn't," the other man said. He sipped from his coffee again and then looked at me. "So what do you do?" he asked.

"I'm a broker," I told him.

He studied my clothes for a moment. "You don't look like a broker," he said.

"I'm on vacation," I told him. I looked at him. "What do you do?"

"Ah, well, this is where things get awkward," he said. He finished the coffee and set the cup down on the floor, then stood up. "I'm a mugger," he said.

I stared at him for a moment, until he pulled a gun out of his jacket pocket and pointed it at me, much like the Elvii were pointing their guns at me.

"Is this some sort of art thing?" I asked him.

"I'm afraid not," he said.

"I don't have any money," I said.

"You're a broker," he said.

"I was just making that up," I told him.

"Why don't you make this easy on the both of us," he said, "and give me your wallet."

I looked around for anyone else but there was no one in sight. "Help!" I called. "I'm being robbed!" My voice echoed through the empty rooms, and then the man hit me across the head with the gun. Suddenly I didn't have control over my body any more. I fell to the floor and curled up in the fetal position.

"I'm sorry about all this," the man said, "but I have a wife and kids to feed." He took my wallet from my pocket and walked away with it, disappearing into the gallery.

I don't know how long I lay there before I could move again. When I touched my forehead, my fingers came away with blood. I heard footsteps and sat up. An old couple with cameras around their necks were wandering through the room, but they stopped when they saw me. I tried to call to them for help, but I could only croak. I waved a bloody hand at them instead.

"Must be one of those performance pieces," the woman said.

The man grunted. "Well, I don't like it," he said. "I don't like it all."

WHEN RACHEL CAME HOME the morning after I was supposed to meet Velma, I was waiting for her. I was wearing my suit, the one I'd bought for all the job interviews I'd never had, and I had the old man's ring in my pocket. I'd lit candles and put them all over the living room, and put a bible on top of the television.

Rachel stopped in the entrance to the living room and stared. "What's all this?" she asked.

I took the ring out of my pocket and held it out to her. She didn't look surprised to see it.

"Is that what you really want?" she asked.

"That's what I really want," I said.

She rubbed her eyes for a moment. "All right then," she said. "All right."

ARE YOU SURE YOU DON'T WANT TO KILL HIM?

I DROVE OVER TO King's place to get back my Tom Waits tickets, the ones he'd stolen out of my wallet. Mia was with me, using the rear-view mirror to put on her makeup. She kept having to redo her lipstick because she'd quit smoking two or three days earlier and now her hands were shaking all the time, like she had a cold. I'd turned up the heat in the car but she'd just rolled the window down. It turned out she'd never been King's girlfriend at all, that she'd just gone to Kennedy's party with him. We were sometimes dating now, but that's another story. She'd come with me because I'd promised to give her one of the tickets.

King lived across the city, on the top floor of a warehouse that had been converted into studio apartments. There was no elevator, so we had to take the stairs. Mia ran all the way up, even though she was wearing a skirt and high heels. By the time I got to the top, she'd already gone into King's place, but I had to stop and catch my breath. There was a band practising in one of the other rooms on the floor, playing the first few bars of the same song over and over. When someone began whistling into a microphone, I followed Mia inside.

The room was mostly empty, just a couple of leather chairs, a stained pool table with one cue lying across it, and a couch that looked as if it had come from Goodwill. King's roommate, Payne, was sitting on it, wearing nothing but a bathrobe that was open at the front. He was staring at Mia, who was pointing a small pistol at him. For some reason, he had an erection.

"What are you doing?" I asked her.

"King's not here," she said, not taking her eyes off Payne. "He's already left."

Payne looked at me and licked his lips but didn't say anything.

I looked around the place. There was another, smaller room off to one side of the main room, and I went in there. The walls were covered in peeling red velvet wallpaper, and there was a bed with black silk sheets in one corner. A framed poster of Audrey Hepburn hung over the head of the bed. I went over to the bed and pulled the sheets off, looked under the mattress. There was nothing but some empty condom wrappers. I emptied the drawers of the dresser onto the floor, kicked through the clothes. Nothing.

"He's not here," I said, walking back into the other room.

"I already told you that," Mia said. She was still pointing the gun at Payne, who still had the erection.

"Where's King?" I asked Payne.

He looked at me with an almost grateful expression. "He's gone for the night. He was going to the Rex, to hustle some guys he knew."

"Did he take the tickets?"

"What tickets?"

"The concert tickets."

"What concert?"

THE THREE OF US were in the car, Payne in the passenger seat. I didn't know where the Rex was, so he was giving me directions.

Mia sat in the back seat. She put the gun against Payne's headrest whenever we stopped at a red light, like he was going to get out and run or something.

"Where did you get that thing anyway?" I asked her. It was shiny and small, the size of her hand.

"I bought it last time I was in New York. Everything is so cheap there."

"Well, don't wave it around in here," I said. "What if it goes off?"

"It won't, it won't."

"But if it does."

"Am I some sort of hostage?" Payne asked.

"No, no, it's nothing like that," I said.

"It's just until we find King," Mia said at the same time.

Payne just looked out the window. It was growing dark, and the sky had turned a violet colour. I looked at my watch. It was nearly eight o'clock. The concert started at nine, but we still had to find a parking spot and get in line.

"What if he's not there?" Payne asked. "What if he's left or something?"

"He'd better be there," Mia warned him. "For your sake."

WE PARKED ON one of the side streets by the Rex and walked back. The place was full of people, every table taken and people standing all the way to the pool tables in the back. The bouncer at the door wanted a five-dollar cover from each of us just to get in. "It's the experimental jazz night," he said, like that explained it all.

"We're just looking for a friend," Mia said. "We'll only be a minute."

The bouncer shook his bald head. "It's five dollars a night or five dollars a minute."

Mia looked at him and then reached into her purse. I didn't know if she was going for money or the gun, so I stopped her. "I've got it," I said and gave the bouncer ten dollars.

"What about him?" he asked, nodding at Payne.

Mia and I both turned to look at Payne. He stood on the sidewalk behind us, arms folded across his chest, shivering. He'd only had time to throw on jeans and a T-shirt before Mia had forced him out the door, and now there was a cold breeze coming down the street. "Well, *I* don't have any money," he said.

I gave the bouncer another five dollars, and he finally stepped out of our way. We went inside.

There must have been a hundred, a hundred and fifty people in there, everyone crowded shoulder to shoulder. I started sweating from the heat almost right away. There was a small stage to one side of the door, empty except for a few stools and a drum set. I got up on it and looked over the crowd but couldn't see King anywhere.

"He's probably at the back," Payne said. "By the pool tables."

I looked that way. I could see the tables, but there was too much smoke in the air to make out anyone's face. "What's he wearing?" I asked Payne.

"How should I know? I'm his roommate, not his girlfriend."

I got down from the stage and started through the crowd. Mia pushed Payne after me. She was shaking hard now, and she looked like she was holding her breath.

"Can someone buy me a drink?" Payne asked. "I think I at least deserve a drink for all this."

There was a tall, skinny man with dreadlocks playing pool by himself at the back. At his feet lay some sort of giant grey dog, panting and watching us approach. There was a line of drool running from its mouth all the way to the floor. I stopped on the other side of the table from the man and watched him sink the five ball with a bank shot. He called it even though he was the only one playing. He waited until the cue ball stopped rolling and then looked up at me.

"You looking to play?"

"Actually, I'm trying to find someone," I said, but now he was looking at Mia, who had pushed past me. "Oh, look at the *puppy!*" she said, bending down to pet the dog.

"I don't think you should do that," I said, but she was already running her hand down the long length of its back. The dog tensed and stared up at her but didn't make a sound.

"Who you looking to find?" the dreadlocked man asked. He was staring at Mia's legs, which were exposed all the way to her upper thighs now that she was bent over.

"It doesn't look like he's here," Payne said to me. "So I think I'm going to leave now."

"I'm trying to find a guy named King," I said, ignoring him. "He's supposed to be playing pool here."

"King?" The man swung his gaze back to me.

"How'd you like to come home with me?" Mia asked the dog. It began to growl at her.

"He's about this high," I said, holding up my hand, "and he's got a scar on his left cheek."

"Right," Payne said.

"What?"

"It's on the right cheek. His scar."

"Whatever."

"One of his girlfriends attacked him with a knife one night."

"*Whatever*," I said.

"Yeah, I've seen him," the dreadlocked man said. He bent over the pool table again and drove the eight ball into one of the pockets without calling it. "He just finished hustling me."

Like that was some sort of cue, the dog launched itself at Mia's throat, snarling and barking. She fell back, screaming and kicking at it. Somehow the dress had ridden all the way up to her hips. She was wearing black silk panties. The dog grabbed on to one of her feet, and she started kicking it in the face with her other foot, while at the same time trying to get her purse open.

I was still wondering what to do when Payne grabbed one of the pool cues from the wall and started beating the dog across the back with it.

"Hey hey *hey*," the dreadlocked man said, coming around the table with his own cue as the dog turned to go after Payne.

I dragged Mia back and then pulled her to her feet. She was digging around inside her purse now, but I grabbed her hand before she could find the gun. "Would you stop that?" I said. I turned around to help Payne, and that's when I saw him. King.

He stepped out of the washroom just as someone started playing guitar onstage. It wasn't any song I recognized, just a bunch of random riffs and notes. He stood there for a moment, looking around, and then glanced our way at Payne's yells. His face was lit up from the washroom's light, and I could see his skin glistening, like he'd just washed it. He looked straight at me. Then he turned and ran for the door.

I went after him. Through the music, I could hear the sounds of Mia's heels on the floor, following me. We went past the bouncer, who was heading for the pool tables now, and out into the night. There was a cab waiting outside, like a getaway car, and King threw himself into the back of it, locked the door.

I hammered on the window and the cabbie took one look at me, then put the car into gear and sped away, tires squealing. King looked back at us and waved.

"We'll get another cab," Mia said, running out into the street and looking around wildly. "We'll chase him, like in the movies."

I pulled her back to the sidewalk and out of the way of a yellow Corvette with its top down. The two men inside — who were both wearing baseball caps — stared at her as they drove past.

"Relax," I told her. "We know where he's going."

The Corvette slowed to a stop in the street and the passenger shouted something at us I couldn't understand.

"Just try it," Mia shouted back. She pulled out the gun and

PLEASE 127

waved it at them. The driver hit the gas, and they disappeared around the corner.

"This is starting to get out of control," I said.

THE CONCERT HALL was only a few blocks away. We were almost there when Mia started laughing. "Oh my God," she said. "We forgot Payne."

It was true. I hadn't even thought about him since I'd seen King. "It doesn't matter," I said. "We didn't need him anyway."

"But we left him with that dog," she said. "You remember it?"

"Oh, I remember."

"And that Jamaican guy. What if he was some sort of crazy dealer or something?"

"What Jamaican guy?" I asked, confused.

"The guy with the hair. And the dog."

"He wasn't Jamaican."

"He wasn't?"

"No. He just had dreadlocks, that's all."

"Well, I think he was crazy anyway. Did you see him go after Payne with that pool cue?"

"It doesn't matter," I said. "Any roommate of King's deserves what he gets."

"But he was helping us," she said, still laughing.

I checked my watch. "There's no way they've opened the doors yet," I said. "King's going to have to wait in line."

Mia laid a hand on my leg. "And you," she said, "you saved my life back there."

"Just let me handle this," I said.

WE PARKED IN A LOT beside the concert hall. There were maybe a hundred people lined up along the sidewalk. A man with a top hat was slowly walking up and down the line, playing an accordion he wore slung over his chest. King was nowhere in sight, so we went up to the front of the line. The doors to the hall were closed and barred with a velvet rope. Two women wearing white shirts and headsets stood in front of the rope, talking in low voices and blowing cigarette smoke away from each other.

"You haven't let anyone in yet, have you?" I asked the women.

Before either of them could answer, the first person in line, a young man wearing a black suit and with slicked-back hair, said, "No budging!"

"Who are you talking to?" Mia asked, looking at him and frowning.

"No one's going in front of me," he said, pointing at us. "I've been here for hours."

"I'm looking for a guy with a scar," I told the women. "On one of his cheeks, I'm not sure which one."

"You've been standing here for hours?" Mia asked. "In that suit?"

"There's a line," he said, flushing. "I was here first."

"I haven't seen anyone with a scar," one of the women said. "Have you?"

"No, no, not on my shift."

"There you go," the first one said.

"And I've been here as long as this guy," the other one told me, nodding at the guy in the suit.

"No one's taking my seat," he said.

"Isn't it assigned seating?" Mia asked.

"It's the principle of the thing!"

We went to the back of the line.

"What if he doesn't show?" Mia wanted to know. "What do we do then?"

"Oh, he'll show," I said.

"But what if he doesn't? How do we get in then?"

"I don't know," I said. "We'll buy some tickets from someone else or something."

"We could shoot our way in," she said. "Like Bonnie and Clyde."

I wasn't listening to her any more, though, because just then King came walking down the sidewalk, a Starbucks coffee in his hand. He stopped at the front of the line and spoke to the women there. I could hear the man in the suit say something about the line.

I grabbed Mia by the hand and pulled her after me. "Whatever you do," I said, "don't kill him."

"All right," she said and giggled.

King was walking down the line now, looking at everyone in the crowd as he passed. "Tickets," he said. "Who needs them?"

"He's selling our tickets," I said. "He's not even going to the concert."

"Are you sure you don't want to kill him?" Mia asked.

We went past the guy playing the accordion. He winked at Mia and nodded at me. Then, as if he sensed us, King looked our way. When he saw me, he stopped moving, stopped blinking even. We were still ten or twelve feet away from him. Then he was pushing through the crowd and running into the parking lot, heading for the street on the far side. I could see more cabs there, so I knew this was our last chance.

I shoved a woman reading a *People* magazine out of the way and went after him. He was fifteen or twenty feet in front of me, winding his way through the cars. I jumped up on the hood of a Lexus and ran across the back of a Mercedes and a Saab to jump down five or six feet behind him. He looked over his shoulder, threw one of the tickets back at me. I stopped to grab it, and when I looked up again, he was almost at the other side of the parking lot.

Then Mia came around a row of parked cars in front of him, the gun in her hand again. She was barefoot and breathing heavily, but grinning. King stopped and put his hands up. She took several steps toward him, the gun pointed at his head.

"Don't shoot him," I yelled, running up to them. I was careful not to step into the line of fire.

"I'm not going to shoot him," Mia said to me, motioning for King to back up. "Not with all these people around."

"Hey," King said weakly. "Come on now."

She walked him behind a nearby trash bin, where no one could see us. Overhead, on the wall of the building, was a large, half-finished mural of a dog holding a giant bone in its mouth.

"Okay, okay, okay," King said, holding out the other ticket. "Let's not get rash here." His face had gone pale except for the scar, which was a red line against his left cheek. Payne had been wrong. "It's all a big misunderstanding ..."

Mia hit him across the face with the gun. He dropped the ticket and sagged back against the wall, the bridge of his nose spilling out blood. "Wait," he said. "Just wait a minute!"

"Yeah, Mia," I said. "What are you doing?"

She hit him again, hard, this time cutting his unscarred cheek. He went down, covering his head with his arms.

"All right then," she said.

"Are you insane?" I asked. I looked around the corner of the trash bin. A couple of people were looking in our direction, but most were still staring ahead, at the doors to the hall. Beside me, Mia bent down to pick up the fallen ticket and then she went through King's pockets. She found a pack of cigarettes in his jacket and lit one. "Thank God," she sighed, leaning back against the wall and closing her eyes.

I looked back at King. He was still covering his head with his arms, but he kept glancing around, like he was trying to find a way out of this situation.

"We have to get out of here," I told Mia. "Before things really get out of hand."

She opened her eyes again, then stepped over to me and took my head in her hands, pulled me into a kiss. Her lips were wet and tasted of smoke. And she was still holding the gun — it was a cold line against the side of my head. I kissed her back. Out of the corner of my eye, I saw King trying to quietly crawl away, leaving a small trail of blood on the pavement behind him. Then I heard one of the women from the concert hall yell that the doors were now open.

It was all I wanted.

HE'LL LIVE FOREVER

I WENT LOOKING FOR EDEN and the hundred dollars he owed me. I'd heard he was shooting a movie downtown. The sky had turned from white to purple before I finally found him, in a little church with yellow police tape covering the doors. When I walked in, he was talking to a young woman with a headset and a clipboard, but he hurried over when he saw me. For some reason he was dressed like Robert Duvall in *Apocalypse Now*, right down to the cavalry hat and sunglasses.

"I thought you were dead," he greeted me.

"I don't think so," I said.

"Yeah, you were definitely dead," he said. He took off his sunglasses to stare at me.

"Well, dead or not, here I am. And I've been looking for you."

"I've been away," he said. "I was shooting a film in Antarctica. It was so cold my piss froze before it hit the ground." He shook his head and put the sunglasses back on. "It's the edge of the fucking world down there, man."

"Where's my hundred dollars?" I asked him, but just then the woman with the clipboard came over.

"Time to work," she said, sliding her arm around his waist. She couldn't have been older than nineteen or twenty. She didn't look at me.

"I can't talk now," Eden told me. "I'm in the middle of a shoot." He pointed at the name tag hanging around his neck. It read Second Assistant Director. His whole life he was never anything but Second Assistant Director. "Thanks for coming by, though," he added.

"I think I'll stick around," I said.

The woman and I sat together in one of the pews. This close I could smell the perfume she wore.

"You a friend of his?" she asked, turning pages on her clipboard.

"We've known each other forever," I said, but she'd stopped listening to me already. Instead, she was leaning forward and whispering something into her headset.

Eden talked to an actor leaning against the altar at the back of the church, then he went over to the camera crew. A bank of lights had been set up outside, shining through one of the stained glass windows, and it turned his skin golden.

When he yelled "Action," the actor, who looked vaguely like someone famous, took a half-dozen steps in our direction. Then a fiery mushroom lifted the altar up and set it on its side. Thunder echoed through the church, and I watched the flames rise up against the ceiling, where they boiled away a painted angel.

When I looked back down, the actor was on fire and flailing away at himself, and Eden was grabbing a fire extinguisher from the camera dolly.

"Is that really someone famous?" I asked the woman beside me, "or is it just a double?"

"That wasn't supposed to happen," she said, frowning.

We watched Eden and the cameraman extinguish the actor, who was screaming hysterically now.

"Was that a real altar?" I asked.

She looked at me for the first time. "Do you really need to be here?" she asked.

Eden came over to us and said, "That wasn't what I wanted at all."

The woman nodded and made a note on her clipboard. "Should we do another take?"

"Does Bob look like he's ready for another take?" Eden asked. We all looked at the actor, who had walked over to us with the help of the cameraman. He looked to be badly burned only on his arms and neck, but his skin all over had the same greasy sheen as barbecued hot dogs. Up close, he didn't look anything like anybody famous.

"My name's Randall," he said. It sounded like he was talking through water.

Eden frowned at him. "No, it's Bob."

"It's Randall," the woman with the clipboard whispered.

Eden was always making mistakes like that. Years later, when the cancer was finally killing him, he got out of his hospital bed and started tearing down all the curtains. "You've set up for the wrong scene," he told the nurses when they tried to stop him.

The doctor told Eden's mother he was delusional. "It's hallucinations caused by the illness," he said.

"If that's so," she answered, "then he's been sick all his life."

Randall started coughing from all the smoke, so we went out to the church steps. Five or six crew members were taking a coffee break there but they left when they saw Eden. He didn't notice because he was taking Randall from the cameraman, who seemed grateful to be rid of him. The cameraman went off after the other crew members, who were watching us from the other side of the police tape now.

"Was it at least a good take?" Randall asked.

"Oh yes, it was very good," the woman said.

"I don't know much about these things," I admitted when he looked at me, "but it certainly looked good from where I was sitting."

"Thank God," Randall said and licked his lips. His tongue was a brilliant pink against his burned lips.

"Well, I guess I'd better call an ambulance," the woman said. She reached for a cell phone on her belt.

Eden put his hand over hers. "Do you have any idea what that would do to our insurance rates?" he asked. "No, he's not hurt that bad."

"Actually," Randall said, "I think I'm hurt really bad."

"I'll drive him to the hospital myself," Eden went on. He offered me his hand. "It was good seeing you again, but I have to get back to work now."

"What about my hundred dollars?" I asked.

Eden looked at the woman. "What is this hundred dollars he keeps going on about?"

"You told me you'd give me a hundred dollars when you had your heart attack," I said.

"Oh, that," Eden said. "It wasn't a heart attack. It was just palpitations."

"That may be," I said, "but I still drove you to the hospital."

"But it wasn't a heart attack," Eden said, frowning.

"I wrecked my car," I said.

"That's right," Eden said. "That's when you got killed."

"We had a deal," I said. "I want my hundred dollars."

Eden looked up at the sky, which was black now, and pushed his hat back. There was a dark rash on his forehead. "I don't have it on me," he said. "I'll have to go to a bank machine."

"I think I'll come along."

We went down the street to Eden's Acura and put Randall in the back seat. The parts of his skin that were burned had already begun to blister, and he smelled like burned rubber. He was still conscious, though, which I figured was a good sign.

"Hang in there, Randy," I said, tightening the seat belt around him. "You'll be as good as new in no time."

"Please don't touch me," he said. "Ah, Christ."

Eden drove us toward the hospital. It was just past nine o'clock, but the day was still like a sauna, the air burning my lungs whenever I took a breath. To make matters worse, the Acura's air conditioning was broken. Randall hooked his fingers into the vent beside him. "Can't you make this thing work?" he pleaded. I leaned out the window to catch the breeze.

We hit a long line of cars and slowed to a stop. Eden pounded the horn. "I hate the summers here," he said. "Every year I think, maybe this is the one where it gets better."

"It never does, though," I said.

"No," he agreed. "But maybe someday."

I looked around the car to pass the time and found some empty pill bottles by my feet. "What are these?" I asked, examining one. They were all unmarked.

"They're for my condition," Eden said.

"What condition?" I asked.

"It's nothing," Eden said. He pounded the horn again.

"Is it anything I could have?" Randall asked. "I'm really hurting here."

Eden searched through his pockets with one hand and came up with another bottle. He passed it to me, and I took out one of the yellow capsules inside.

"What do they do?" Randall asked.

"They make you feel like you're coming apart," Eden said. "But they take care of the pain."

I reached back and laid the capsule on Randall's tongue, then watched him as he tried to swallow it.

"You can have one, too, if you like," Eden said to me.

"No thanks," I said. "I'm done with all that."

Just then Randall caught sight of himself in the rear-view mirror. "Is that me?" he asked.

"I'm afraid so," I told him.

"For Christ's sake," he said, raising his hands to the burned parts of his face and neck. "Look at me! I'm ruined!"

"It's not that bad," Eden said. He pounded the horn again.

Randall looked like he wanted to cry, but I think all the moisture in his eyes had dried up. "I'm supposed to work on a fucking *HBO* film next month. How am I supposed to do that with a face like this?"

"These things happen," Eden said.

"I look like a mutant! Like the Elephant Man or something!"

"You'll move on."

"I'll fucking sue!"

"Yeah yeah yeah."

After a while the traffic started rolling again. We were driving past the police station when Eden suddenly jammed both feet down on the brake pedal. "Jesus Christ, it's John Cusack!"

"Where?" Randall and I both asked, but Eden was already pulling a U-turn onto the other side of the street. "The blue Beamer two cars ahead," he said, ignoring the horns sounding all around us.

"What are you doing?" I said. "We have to get my hundred dollars. We have to get Randall here to the hospital."

"That's right," Randall sighed.

"Get the script," Eden said.

"The script?" I looked around the car until he pointed at the glove compartment. When I opened it, a stack of water-stained papers fell out.

"I've been trying to get it to John for years," he said. "I wrote it with him in mind."

"What is it?" I asked.

"It's an action adventure crossed with a black comedy. Like *Grosse Point Blank* meeting the Coen brothers in their *Barton Fink* stage."

I glanced at the first few pages. Poor Eden. Even back then it was clear he was never going to be anybody. "I don't know about this," I said.

But Eden wasn't paying attention any more. He'd managed to get behind the BMW and now he stuck his head out the window. "Johnnie!" he yelled. "Hey, Johnnie, it's me!"

Ahead of us the BMW driver stepped on it. Eden put both feet on the gas pedal and followed.

"You really know him?" I asked.

"No," Eden admitted, "but it was worth a try." He reached under his seat and pulled out a camcorder. "Here," he said, handing it to me. "You might as well film this. We might be able to use it later."

I leaned out the window again, enjoying the wind now that we were driving fast, and focused the camera on the car ahead of us. "Are you sure it's him?" I asked.

"Oh, it's John all right."

We chased the BMW through the city, recklessly passing cars in both lanes and running red lights. It was like we were in a movie ourselves. I turned the camera on Eden. "So tell me, Eden," I said, "why do you want him to have this script?"

"Well, that's a bit of a stupid question," Eden said. "I mean, if I wrote the script with him in mind, then doesn't it stand to reason I'd want him to see it?"

"What if he doesn't take it?" I asked, but he wouldn't answer me.

Then we were in Chinatown, and I was filming the passing shops. There were lights everywhere, and the rushing air smelled like bread. "Can I have a part in your film?" I asked. "You can forget about the hundred bucks if you give me a part in the film."

But Eden didn't answer, because he was hitting the brakes. "Oh shit!" he said.

Twenty feet in front of us, the BMW was trapped behind a line of cars at a red light. Cusack got out, one of those club things for locking steering wheels in his hand. Everything was in slow motion. Eden drove around the side of the BMW to stop from hitting it, and Cusack put up his hand. He opened his mouth wide just before we drove into him.

"Shit!" Eden said again as Cusack disappeared under the front of the Acura, one hand briefly clawing at the hood. We came to a stop. "I just killed John Cusack," Eden said. Then he jumped out and ran around to the front of the car. I reached over and put the car into park before going after him. Most of the people at the stalls beside us turned to watch, and I made sure I got a good crowd shot. The smell of bread was gone now, replaced by that of rotten vegetables.

"Is he really dead?" I asked, stopping beside Eden and turning the camera on the fallen man.

"This isn't John Cusack," Eden said.

I zoomed in on the other man. It was true. He had dark hair, but other than that he didn't look anything like Cusack. He stared up at us, his mouth pushing out little pink bubbles. His body looked broken in ways I hadn't been able to imagine before.

"I don't know what I was thinking," Eden added.

"I told you," I said.

"This isn't the time for that."

"We should really get out of here," I said. But it was already too late. A cop pulled up then, parking behind the Acura. He had one of those little cameras mounted on his dash, and I filmed it filming us.

The cop talked into his radio for a moment, then got out and started walking toward us. He stopped for a long moment to look at Randall, who'd passed out against the window. "What happened to this guy?" he asked.

"It's all right," I said, "he's an actor."

The cop stared at Randall for a moment longer, then came over to stand beside us. All three of us looked down at the other man. An escaped crab scuttled past our feet, under the car.

"Which one of you was driving?" the cop asked. He scratched the back of his neck and belched softly.

"I was," Eden sighed.

The cop shook his head. "You'd be the one in a world of trouble then." He took out his notepad and started writing.

"Shouldn't you be doing something?" I asked him, pointing at the man on the ground.

"Somebody will be along shortly," he said.

Eden sat on the ground and tore off his cavalry hat. I saw his whole head was covered in that rash. "Why is this always happening to me?" he asked, starting to cry.

What could I do? I went over and sat beside him, put my arm around his shoulder. Together we watched the other man. He wasn't blinking any more, and he only took a breath every now and then. I turned off the camera and put it on the ground.

I was never going to see my hundred dollars again.

Later, when the ambulance had arrived, the cop made Eden get into the back seat of his cruiser.

"Do you think he's going to be all right?" Eden asked, still looking at the fallen man.

"Oh yeah," the cop laughed, just before he shut the door. "He'll live forever."

HELL BELIEVES IN YOU

LOOKING BACK ON IT NOW, I think it was the Mormons who robbed me. The two of them had been wandering around the neighbourhood for a couple of days before it happened, knocking on doors, seeing who was home and who wasn't. They even had little pads of paper that they made notes on. I knew they were Mormons because they wore white shirts and those black name tags.

One morning they came to my house. They were both wearing sunglasses. I couldn't see anything but my own reflection in them. "We'd like to talk to you about Hell," the one on the left said when I answered the door. He smiled like there wasn't anything else he'd rather be talking about.

"I don't really believe in Hell," I told him.

He looked over my shoulder, into my apartment. I could smell cigarette smoke on him now. "If we could just come in for a moment," he said.

"I'm just on my way to work," I told them.

"When's a good time for us to come back?" he asked.

"I work all the time," I said.

I started to close the door, but the other Mormon stopped it with his foot. "It doesn't matter whether you believe in Hell," he said. "Hell believes in you."

I ACTUALLY WAS WORKING during this time, as an enumerator. It was a temporary sort of thing I found through the paper. My job was to knock on people's doors and register them to vote. I was working with a man named Lincoln. It was the kind of job one person could do, but they made us work in pairs anyway. The woman who hired me said that people were more willing to open the door to pairs than to individuals.

Sometimes Lincoln talked about the neighbourhood where he lived. "It's all students," he told me one time. "Every time I walk out the door, I'm reminded of all the ways my life has gone wrong since I left school. But the rent is cheap."

"I could never live like a student again," I told him.

"I don't live *like* a student," he said. "I live in the same neighbourhood as students."

"What's the difference?" I asked.

"And there are benefits," he went on. "The woman who lives across the street doesn't have any blinds."

"Why not?" I asked.

"How should I know?" he said. "Maybe she can't afford them, or maybe she just likes people looking at her. Anyway, the point is that I can watch her any time I want."

"Does she change in front of her windows?" I asked.

"No, it's nothing like that," he said. "I just watch her doing her regular house stuff. You know, cooking dinner, talking on the phone, that kind of thing."

"So you don't watch her change?" I asked.

"Well, sometimes," he admitted, "but that's not really what I'm interested in."

"There's something not right with you," I told him.

WE MET ALL SORTS working that job. One man invited us in for beer. He looked like the kind of guy who played hockey every week. His furniture was all black leather. We sat at his kitchen table and did the paperwork there. Some sort of Christian talk show was coming from the radio. The voices were low and soothing. The table was already covered with empty beer bottles even though it was only noon.

When I asked the man how many people lived there, he stared out the window, into his backyard. There was a riding lawn mower parked in the middle of the yard. Half the lawn was cut and the rest was overgrown.

"I'm not sure," he finally said.

"You don't know how many people live here?" I asked him.

"It used to be me and my wife," he said, "but now ... I just don't know any more."

"Well, we can only enter definite residents," I told him, "so I'll just put down one."

He didn't say anything else, didn't even move for a moment. Then he put his face in his hands and started to cry.

Lincoln and I got up and went back outside. The man followed us, still crying. "You haven't finished your beers," he said through his tears. "You have to stay and finish your beers."

"We're working," I told him as I went down the steps of his porch. "We have jobs to do."

ANOTHER TIME WE walked past a man who was dying, although we didn't know he was dying at the time. He was on the other side of the street, leaning on the inside of the white wooden fence surrounding his yard. He waved at us with a handful of mail, and

I waved back, kept on walking. It was only when we went down the other side of the street, maybe fifteen minutes later, that I saw he was dead.

He was lying face down in the grass, the letters scattered around him. The wind had blown a postcard underneath the fence and onto the sidewalk at our feet. I could see ants crawling around the top of his bald head already.

"I'm guessing a heart attack," Lincoln said, looking down at him. "What do you think?"

"I think we'd better do something," I said.

"Do you know CPR?" Lincoln asked.

"I've been meaning to take one of those courses," I said, "but I just never got around to it."

"We'd better not do anything then," he said. "We could make things worse."

"He's not breathing," I said. "How worse can it get?"

"I meant worse for us," he said.

"Well, we can't just stand here," I said. "We're government employees. We have to do something." I went to walk through the gate, but Lincoln stopped me. "He's on private property," he said. "Think of the lawsuits." He took out his cell phone and called an ambulance. "We'll let someone else worry about it," he told me when he was done.

I reached down and picked up the postcard while we waited for the ambulance to arrive. The front was a picture of the Eiffel Tower. On the back someone had written in red ink: "Hi Mom and Dad! Last stop! See you soon! Love, Kathy!"

When the ambulance arrived, the paramedics didn't even look at us. They knelt beside the man at the same time the door of the house opened and a woman stepped out. She was wearing a housecoat and holding a cup of coffee in her hand. She looked at the ambulance, at us standing there, and then at the dead man and the paramedics. "Oh my *God*," she said and dropped the coffee cup. It broke at her feet, and the coffee sprayed as far as the dead man. I dropped the postcard back to the ground. I don't think she noticed me reading it.

"We'd better come back for this one later," Lincoln said.

IT WAS ONLY AFTER we'd done a few more houses that I remembered. "Oh my God," I said. "I waved at him."

"What are you talking about?" Lincoln asked, looking around the street. "Waved at who?"

"That dead man," I said. "He was trying to get our attention and all I did was wave at him."

"How were you supposed to know?"

"Imagine that," I said. "You're dying, and the last thing you see is me waving at you."

"It's sure not what I'd want to see in that situation," Lincoln said.

"This is going to haunt me forever," I said.

"Well, don't let it get you down," he said. "We're on a schedule here."

IT WAS AFTER THIS that the break-ins started. I came home one day after work to find my door unlocked and a half-eaten sandwich and a cigarette butt in the sink. Neither had been there when I'd left that morning. And I didn't smoke anyway.

I went around my apartment with the only knife I owned, a small steak knife with a broken tip. I looked in all the rooms and closets, but I couldn't see any other signs of anyone else having been there. And nothing had been taken. Whoever it was that had broken in had made themselves a sandwich, smoked the cigarette, and then left.

I phoned my landlord. He was a lawyer who owned buildings all over the city. I'd never actually seen him, as he'd sent his secretary over to show me around the place.

"Were you in my apartment today?" I asked him.

"Why would I want to go into your apartment?" he asked.

"Well, someone was in here today while I was gone," I told him. "They made a sandwich and had a cigarette."

"People shouldn't be smoking in there," he said. "It stains the walls."

"I'm concerned someone might have an extra key," I said. "Or maybe the lock is easy to pick."

"I guess you'd better change your lock then," he said.

"I was kind of hoping you'd do that," I said.

"It's not in our agreement," he pointed out.

"How much would another lock cost me?" I asked.

"I don't know," he said. "Fifty or sixty bucks, plus labour."

"Well, maybe they won't come back," I said.

I WENT BACK to the dead man's house after work one day and rang the doorbell. The same woman answered the door, still in her housecoat. Her eyes were so red it looked as if all the blood vessels in them had burst. She stared at me like she had no idea who I was until I said, "I was here when your husband died."

She looked at me a moment longer, then said, "You called the ambulance."

"Well, I was with the man who called the ambulance," I said, but she was already walking back into the house. "I've just put some coffee on," she called over her shoulder.

I followed her down the hall to her kitchen. The walls of the hall were lined with framed family photographs. I tried not to look at any of them.

The woman sat me down at a wooden table in the kitchen and poured me a cup of coffee. There was a bowl of apples in the middle of the table, with unopened letters piled around it. I saw the postcard I'd read underneath one of the envelopes.

The woman sat down across from me, picked an apple out of the bowl and started polishing it on her housecoat. I tried the coffee. It was strong and bitter, but I didn't say anything. Fruit flies drifted around my face.

"Well," the woman finally said. "What can I do for you?"

"I wanted to apologize," I said. "About your husband's death ..."

"That's very kind of you," she said. She put the apple back in the bowl and took out another one. They all looked polished to me already.

"No, that's not what I meant," I said. "I meant, I wish I could have done more."

"He had a bad heart," she said. "There's nothing anyone could have done."

"He waved at me," I told her. "I didn't know what he wanted."

She paused in polishing the apple for a second, then resumed, but slower. "What do you mean?" she asked.

"I just waved back," I went on. "I didn't know."

"What are you trying to tell me?" she asked.

"I don't know," I said. "Maybe I could have saved him."

She put the apple back in the bowl but didn't take another one.

"If I would have known," I said.

"What do you want from me?" she asked.

"I don't know," I said.

"Get out," she told me.

"I just wanted you to know I wish I could have done more."

She got up and came around the table. I thought she was going to hit me, but instead she picked up my coffee cup and went over to the sink with it. "Get out," she said again and emptied the cup into the sink.

AT NIGHT I DREAMED about the people we'd enumerated that day. Only now they were all dead, like zombies. They opened the doors to their houses and shuffled down the sidewalk after me, worms writhing in their eye sockets. And when they met each other in the street they fought, tearing into each other with their teeth and ripping each other's limbs off. The streets ran with blood. It was so deep I had to wade through it. And the more they killed each other, the deeper it got, until it was flowing into their houses and threatening to drown me.

It was the same thing every night.

THE SECOND TIME my place was broken into, they made sandwiches again, but this time they also took all my CDs and videos. I went around the apartment but couldn't find anything else missing. I called the police this time.

A single cop showed up an hour later. He wandered around the apartment, making notes in a little black book and looking at all the photos on my wall.

"Aren't you going to dust for fingerprints or anything like that?" I asked.

"For some CDs and videos?" he asked and shook his head. He stopped by my bookshelf and studied the books on it.

"How are you going to catch these guys then?" I wanted to know.

"We usually don't," he admitted. "Unless you have an idea of who might have done it?" He looked at me.

"If I knew that," I said, "do you think I would have called you?"

"Well, you'll probably want to change your locks," he said. "Sometimes they come back."

"Tell me something I don't know," I told him.

ONE OF THE HOUSES in the neighbourhood we worked was home to a psychic. It was an old Victorian house with a hand-painted sign in the window — Palms Read, Fortunes Told. Lincoln stayed on the porch, smoking a cigarette, while I went inside.

The room I walked into looked like an office. There was a white leather couch under the window and a wooden desk and chairs on the other side of the room. A crystal ball sat on one corner of the desk. There was another door behind the desk but it was closed.

I sat on the couch and waited, but no one came into the room. After a few minutes, I got up and went through the closed door. There was a kitchen on the other side. Rows of dirty glasses sat on one side of the sink, stacks of dirty plates on the other. Pizza boxes covered the table, and a man's voice came from the radio on the counter. "The signs are all there in the Book of Revelations," he said. "There's a purging fire coming, my friends, but those who do the right thing in God's eyes will have nothing to fear." The air smelled of mould in here.

A toilet flushed somewhere nearby, and then a door I hadn't noticed near the kitchen table opened. A woman with grey hair and jowls came out of the bathroom. She wore the kind of dress that only old European women wear. She closed the door behind her and then stopped, looked at me standing in her kitchen.

"I need to ask you some questions," I told her.

We went back into the other room and filled out the enumeration forms. When we finished, Lincoln was smoking another cigarette. I kept sitting there, and the woman asked, "Is there anything else?"

"I'm having some problems at home," I said. "I was hoping you could help me."

She reached into a drawer of the desk and pulled out a deck of tarot cards. "Problems with your love life? Financial problems?"

"I want to find out who's breaking into my apartment," I said.

She put the cards back in the drawer. "I can't answer that with these," she said.

"What about that?" I asked, pointing at the crystal ball. "Can you see who's breaking into my apartment with that?"

"This?" She picked up the ball and shook it. The inside of it filled with snow. "This is just a prop," she said.

"Well, what can you tell me then?" I asked.

"I read fortunes," she said. "I can tell you what's going to happen to you in the future."

"Like if I'm going to die?" I asked. "That kind of thing?"

"Of course you're going to die," she said. "You don't need me to tell you that."

THE THIRD TIME they broke into my apartment, they took everything, even the furniture. The place was completely empty, not even blinds for the windows. It was like I had never lived there at all. I couldn't even call the police because they'd taken my phone.

There was a pamphlet from the Mormons in my mailbox. Sorry We Missed You. The words were superimposed over a picture of a burning lake with hands sticking up through the flames.

I WENT OVER TO Lincoln's place after work one night for a game of poker. There were four of us playing: Lincoln, myself, a man named Wylie, and another, older man named Butler. A fifth man, Sinnet, had called and canceled. "He's having problems with his wife," Lincoln said when he put down the phone. "She said she was going to have an affair if he went out tonight." He laughed, like the idea pleased him.

We were playing at Lincoln's kitchen table. It was low-stakes poker, quarter ante. The highest pot so far had been five dollars, which I had won on a straight. Lincoln had to tell me I'd won, because I still didn't know which hands were higher. I'd come over with twenty dollars and now I had thirty, but most of it was in change. Lincoln had a big jar full of quarters with which he made change for the bills. It looked like the kind of jar they store fetuses and dead animals in.

I was telling everyone about the dead man we'd seen. "He was just lying there," I said, "like he was sleeping. I was going to give him mouth-to-mouth or something, but Lincoln stopped me."

The other two men looked at Lincoln. "The guy was dead," he said, dealing a fresh hand. "There was no point wasting energy on him."

"Well, if he was already dead," Wylie said.

"I still wanted to try and save him, though," I said. "So then I could say to people, well, at least I didn't just stand around and do nothing."

"You would have been sued," Lincoln said.

"Why would someone sue me for that?" I shook my head.

"Why wouldn't they?" Wylie said.

"I thought I was having a heart attack once," Butler said. "It was just some sort of weird palpitations, though. But my wife, she didn't do a damned thing. Just sat there and watched. When it stopped, I said, what the hell are you doing? Were you waiting for me to die?"

"Was she?" Wylie asked.

"I don't know. She told me she was paralyzed with fright." He shook his head. "I was the one who was goddamned well paralyzed with fright."

"Which wife was that?" Wylie asked.

"Does it matter?" Butler said.

"You in or out?" Lincoln asked me.

I looked at my cards. I had a pair of tens, an ace, and a pair of kings. I had no idea if that was good or not. There was ten dollars in the pot.

"I'm in," I said.

"Then add your dollar."

I did, and so did Butler, and now there was twelve dollars in the pot.

"I saw a cyclist get killed once," Wylie said. "Had his head down and rode straight into a bus that was turning. Cracked his head wide open. You could see his brain." He shook his head. "I'm not afraid of dying, but I am afraid of dying stupidly."

"What did his brain look like?" Lincoln asked.

"Just like on television."

"Did he have a helmet on?" I asked.

"Does it sound like he had a helmet on? Besides, the impact

broke his neck. He would have been one of those — what's the term for it?" He looked at Butler.

"A quad," Butler said.

"Right."

"But at least he'd be alive," I said.

"I'd sooner have people looking into the inside of my dead head," Wylie said, "than staring at my drooling, twitching face."

"I think I'll call," Butler said.

We all laid our cards on the table. Butler sighed.

"Looks like you win again," Wylie said, leaning over to look at my cards.

"Looks like you need another beer," Butler told me and went over to the fridge. He never got the beer, though. Instead, he stopped by the kitchen window and said, "Your neighbour is on fire." He stayed there, looking out the window.

"What?" Lincoln and I asked at the same time. Wylie was in the middle of lighting a cigarette so he didn't say anything.

"The place across the street," Butler said. "It's on fire." He turned the kitchen sink tap on and let the water run, like that would help.

The rest of us stood up and went over to the window. We looked through our reflections at the house across the street. All the lights were off, but there were flames shooting through the blinds in one of the second-floor windows.

"Is that where the woman you watch lives?" I asked Lincoln. He didn't answer, though, because he was already running for the door. The rest of us followed him.

"What do you mean, the woman he watches?" Butler asked as we went outside.

"It's hard to explain," I told him. "And I'm not really sure I understand it anyway."

I could smell the smoke as soon as I was outside, but I couldn't hear a thing. Fires always made a lot of noise in the movies, but this one was so quiet I could hear someone laughing in one of the houses next door. I followed Lincoln across the street and up the house's steps, to the front door. He had his cell phone out and was calling 911 now. I knocked on the door, then tried the handle when there was no answer. The door was locked.

"What are you doing?" Lincoln asked, putting the phone back into his pocket.

"I was checking to see if anyone was home," I said.

"If anyone was home," he said, "I think they'd be putting out the fire, not coming to see who was at the door."

"Well, we can't just stand around doing nothing again," I said.

"What are you talking about?"

"This is our chance to do something right." I kicked the door just underneath the handle a couple of times, and there was a loud crack as the frame splintered. I pushed the door open and went inside, Lincoln following after me.

We were in a living room with stairs running up one wall. I could hear the fire now, burning somewhere near the top of the stairs, and the air was hazy with smoke. Lincoln turned on the light, and I paused a moment to look around. There was a framed Warhol Marilyn Monroe on one wall, dozens of framed photographs along another.

"Hello?" I called. "Anyone home?"

When no one answered, Lincoln asked, "Now what?"

"Give me a hand with this," I said, going over to the television. I was coughing from the smoke now.

We carried the television outside and set it down on the lawn. Both Butler and Wylie were standing on the sidewalk, watching. Neither one of them moved in our direction. "Help us out here," I said, but they just shook their heads.

"That place is on fire," Butler said. "I'm not going in there."

"It's not safe," Wylie added.

"I'm going for another beer," Butler said. "Anyone else want one?"

"You might as well bring them all," Lincoln said, coming out with the telephone and a handful of CDs.

Thick smoke was starting to flow down the stairs by the time Lincoln and I carried the couch out, and we could hear sirens in the distance. Most of the woman's living room was scattered around the front yard by this point. Wylie and Butler were sitting on the coffee table, drinking the beer they'd brought from Lincoln's place. There was still no one else on the street, but I could see faces looking out at us from the neighbouring houses now that the flames were coming out of all the upstairs windows.

"That's it," Lincoln said, dropping his end of the couch and sitting on it. He couldn't stop coughing, and his skin was black with ash and sweat. "I think I've reached my limit here," he gasped.

I started moving the furniture around the lawn, dragging the couch and chairs into the same arrangement they'd had inside the house. That was when the fire truck arrived. Two firemen wearing oxygen masks and carrying axes walked over and watched me for a moment. "What the hell are you doing?" one of them asked.

"I'm just trying to help," I said.

"Get the hell out of here!" he shouted, waving his axe at me. I went over to stand beside Butler and Wylie, who had moved from the coffee table to the sidewalk when the fire truck pulled up. Lincoln stood up from the couch and then bent over, started vomiting on his feet. Wylie handed me a beer. "They're a little warm," he said. "On account of the fire." I drank half of it down in one swallow, then the three of us watched the firemen drag hoses into the burning house.

By the time we'd finished the beer, the fire was out. The firemen came out of the house and sat on the bumpers of their truck while a cop sealed off the entrance of the house with yellow tape. I went over and sat beside Lincoln on the couch.

"I don't think I'm going to make it into work tomorrow," he

said. His chin and the front of his shirt were streaked with a mixture of vomit and soot.

"Well, that's all right," I said. I put my feet up on the coffee table and looked around the yard. "We certainly did a good job here."

"We did," Lincoln agreed.

"Redemptive, even."

"I don't know what that word means."

"She won't even be able to tell the difference when she comes home," I said.

"I'm not so sure about that."

I sat for hours on the couch after the others went back inside to finish the poker game. I was waiting for her to come home, so I could tell her that I was the one who'd brought everything outside and saved it from the fire. I kept on waiting even after Butler and Wylie drove away with a wave at me, and after Lincoln's lights went out. But she didn't come home that night. She never found out what I did.

HOW LONG DOES THIS SORT OF THING USUALLY TAKE?

AND THIS IS THE STORY of the last time I ever saw Rachel.

I had to take her to the clinic. I was watching television in the living room while I waited for her to get dressed. There was a documentary on, something about a village in Mongolia where all the women wore white T-shirts with Tide logos on them. Boxes of Tide were everywhere, in the baskets they carried, in front of stores, in the doorways of huts. The narrator said they even brushed their teeth with the stuff.

"Think of what that would do to your insides if you swallowed it," I yelled to Rachel in the other room. When she didn't answer, I added, "Why Tide? Why not Arm and Hammer? Or ABC?"

"Maybe they worship Tide," she said, coming out of the bedroom. "Maybe it's like some sort of god to them." She was dressed in sweat pants and a T-shirt, like she was just going out for a jog.

"I don't think so," I said.

"This kind of thing happens all the time," she went on. "Remember that tribe in Africa or New Zealand or wherever it was that worshipped Coke bottles?"

"I think that was a movie," I said, "not real life."

"Oh no," she said, "it's all real-life."

OUTSIDE, IT HAD RAINED all night, and now the air was cold and wet, like the inside of a forest. There were earthworms everywhere, curling themselves into little knots or trying to dig their way into the sidewalk. I stepped over them carefully, but Rachel put her feet down without looking.

I once lived with a Jamaican guy who wouldn't go out in rainstorms because of the worms. "How can you stand it?" he'd asked me one time. "All those maggots coming out of the ground like that?"

"Worms," I'd corrected him. "They're worms, not maggots."

"What's the difference?" he'd asked. "I get sick just thinking about it."

He'd been living with me because his wife had kicked him out. He later wound up in jail for hitting her, although I should point out that she had driven their car into him first. He told the judge at the trial that he just wanted a happy marriage, like on television. He got six months.

We found my car around the corner and drove along the wet streets, accompanied only by the sounds of the engine and the squeal of the brakes whenever we took a corner. I tried the radio after a few minutes, but it was still broken.

"How long does this sort of thing usually take?" I asked after a while.

Rachel looked out the side window and didn't answer me right away, and for a moment I thought maybe she was crying. I looked closely at her, afraid I'd see tears on her cheeks, but there was nothing on her face at all.

"I don't know," she finally said. "I don't do this all that often."

THE LAST TIME I'd been in a clinic had been months before I'd met Rachel. I'd gone because I'd woken up that morning with an itching I was convinced was gonorrhea or syphilis or something like that.

The doctor was less convinced, though. He didn't bother to sit down when he came into the examination room, just leaned against the desk and stared over my head, at a poster of internal organs taped to the wall. He didn't look me in the eye the whole time I was there.

"You been having sex recently?" he asked.

"No, I've given up on all that," I said.

"What about coffee or alcohol? You been drinking a lot lately?"

"I guess. No more than usual, though."

"It's probably just an infection then, but we'll do some blood tests anyway," he said. He had me lower my pants and lie down on the examination table. I thought very hard about not getting an erection as he touched me, but it was already too late.

"Well, at least everything's working fine," he commented.

"This doesn't usually happen," I said.

"That's all right. Lets me see things easier."

I thought about killing him then, about knocking him to the floor and searching through his drawers until I found a hypodermic or scalpel I could stab him with. Or maybe I could strangle him with the cord of that thing they use to look in your ears.

Thinking about all that just made me harder, though, and I swore then that I was never going to set foot in such a place again.

RACHEL AND I FOUND a walk-in clinic by the twenty-four-hour A&P. Inside the clinic, the walls were covered in half-finished murals of Winnie the Pooh and Tigger. No signs of the others, though, no Piglet or Christopher Robin. On the television in the corner, Oprah was talking to the empty waiting room.

The nurse at the reception desk was reading a *Cosmopolitan* magazine and didn't look away from it when we walked up. "Reason for visit?" she asked, circling the answers to a quiz.

"I need a morning-after pill," Rachel told her.

Now the nurse looked at me, and I felt I had to say something. "The condom broke," I explained. "But I didn't notice until afterwards."

"You should always buy the extra-strong ones," the nurse said. "Just in case." She gave Rachel some paperwork to fill out and then went back to her quiz.

We sat in the waiting room and watched *Oprah*. It was a rerun about parents reuniting with the children they'd given up for adoption. Everybody was crying, but I couldn't concentrate. I didn't understand why we had to wait when we were the only people in the place.

"Christ," Rachel said, shaking her head at the television. "Isn't there anything else on?"

I looked around for the remote but didn't see it anywhere. I went up to the counter and asked the nurse if she had it.

"We lost it," she told me, not looking up from the magazine again. "We think maybe one of the patients stole it."

"Why don't you just get a new one?" I asked her.

"That was the new one," she said.

I went over to the television to try and turn the channel, but it was too high on the wall for me. I even tried jumping, which made Rachel laugh.

"I can't watch any more of this," she said. "I'm going outside for some air."

When she didn't come back, I began to wonder if she'd left, so I followed her. She was lying on the trunk of my car, smoking a cigarette. It was starting to rain again, but she didn't seem to care. She just kept lying there, staring up at the sky.

"What's wrong with you?" I asked.

She shook her head. "Nothing," she said. "There's nothing wrong with me."

LATER. IN THE EXAMINATION room down the hall, I found a stack of brochures about pregnancy.

"It says here that all the cells are identical in the first two weeks," I told Rachel, showing her the pictures. "It's only later that they start changing into different parts of the body."

"I really don't want to hear this right now," she said.

"But they start growing right away. It could be growing inside you right now."

"I'm never having sex with you again," she told me.

Just then the doctor came in. She looked like somebody's mother, with her gray hair and floral blouse. She sat down at the desk and took a package of pills from her pocket.

"You'll need to take two right away," she told Rachel, "and you can't eat anything for twenty-four hours."

"Right, right," Rachel said.

"Are you sure about this?" I asked her, and now the doctor looked at me for the first time.

"Sure about what?" Rachel asked.

"Maybe we should just wait and see what happens," I said.

"Out of all our choices," she said, "I think that's about last on the list."

"Will it at least kill the baby fast then?" I asked the doctor. "Before it starts growing a brain or anything?"

"I think we're about done here," she said.

Rachel dry-swallowed two of the pills. She closed her eyes for a moment, then opened them and smiled at me. "I can feel them working already," she said.

I WAITED IN THE CAR while Rachel finished talking to the doctor. I was spending the whole night waiting. After a while, I started thumping the steering wheel with my fists. I couldn't stop until Rachel finally came out.

She stood in the doorway for a moment and lit another cigarette before coming over to the car. She opened the door but didn't get in, just stood there, smoking and looking around the empty lot.

"Everything okay?" I asked.

"Everything's fine now," she said. She laughed. "That was a close one."

I sat there a moment longer and then said, "What do we do now?"

"We need groceries," she said, looking at the A&P.

"All right." I started to get out of the car.

"I'd like to do it on my own," she said. She flicked the cigarette away without extinguishing it.

"I'll wait here," I said.

ONCE RACHEL WAS INSIDE the A&P, I started the car and drove a few streets over, to an all-night gas station I knew about. The attendant, a young man named Phil, topped up the gas tank and then leaned into my window.

"You sure picked the right night," he said, rubbing his nose with an oil-stained finger. "A friend of mine who works at the hospital just dropped off some meds."

"What do they do?" I asked.

"I'm not really sure," he admitted. "But he told me they use them to calm down the crazies."

"That sounds just fine," I said.

He slapped the car's roof and went back inside. I sat there and watched the traffic pass. A cop cruised past once but he never looked my way. Still, I was sweating by the time Phil finally came back.

He counted my money twice and then handed over a baggie holding a half-dozen yellow-and-black capsules. I dry-swallowed one right away and threw the rest in the glove compartment. The one I'd swallowed scratched my throat all the way down.

"You want anything else?" Phil asked. "Oil checked or anything like that?"

"No, that's all I need."

"We've got windshield washer fluid on sale."

I STARTED TO GET HUNGRY on the way back to the A&P. I took a few more of the pills, but they didn't help. I drove around the area for a while, looking for a coffee shop that was still open, but there was nothing, just lit-up, empty office buildings. I couldn't even find a 7-Eleven.

I stopped at a red light, and that's when the drugs hit me. I felt like I was slowly collapsing inward. When the light turned green again, I couldn't bring myself to touch the gas pedal. I couldn't even take my foot off the brake. I just sat there, staring at the light as it changed colours what seemed once every hour or so.

After a while, I noticed more lights flashing on and off behind me, but I didn't see the cop until he rapped on my door with his flashlight. Then I saw the cruiser in the rear-view. I somehow managed to roll down the window.

"What are you doing?" the cop asked me. He was an older man, tall and heavy and with a white mustache. The hand not holding the flashlight was on his gun.

I stared at him. "What do you mean?" I finally managed.

"What do you think I mean?" he asked me.

I thought that over for a moment and then said, "I was just on my way to pick up my wife. She's doing a little shopping."

"Did you know your lights are off?" he asked me.

"No, I didn't," I said. I looked around the deserted street. I couldn't see what difference it made whether my lights were on or not. There were streetlights everywhere, after all.

"Did you also know that you haven't moved in the last five minutes?" he went on. His voice was quiet and conversational.

"I'd like to," I said, "but I really can't."

"What do you mean, you can't?"

"I don't know. I just can't."

He looked at me for a moment longer, then said, "Wait here."

"All right," I said. Where did he think I would go?

He walked back to his car and spoke into his radio for a while. When he came back, he opened my door and reached in to turn off the ignition. "Seeing as you can't drive," he said in that same tone of voice, "I'm going to do it for you." I let him walk me back to his cruiser. Once he had me on my feet and was guiding me, I could move just fine. But what I really wanted to do was sit down and not move at all.

We waited for a tow truck to come for my car, and then he took me to a hospital I'd never been to before. I couldn't take my eyes off the doctor who examined me. He was young and clean-shaven, with hair that shone under the fluorescent lights. Behind him, the walls burned with more light, like it was seeping through from the other side. I understood then what the cop had meant about my lights being out. He'd brought me here so I could shine like this young doctor.

"I found these in the car," the cop told the doctor, showing him the bag of pills. I hadn't seen him take them, hadn't even noticed him searching the car, but that was okay. I didn't want any more of those pills.

"How many of these did you take?" the doctor asked me, holding up the bag and frowning at its contents.

"I don't know," I said. "Three or four."

"Jesus," the doctor said.

"Is he going to be all right?" the cop asked.

"Probably. Physically, anyway."

They put me into a room with an old woman in the bed opposite mine. There were tubes sticking out of her nose and arms, and she only breathed every few seconds or so. There seemed to be a longer gap between each breath. It occurred to me that she was probably dying.

I looked out the window. Somehow the sky had already lightened into grey. I couldn't see the street outside, but I could hear the cars driving by. All those people, going on with their lives, and there I was, lying in a room with a dying woman.

I don't know how long I lay there before the nurse came in. She looked at the old woman and shook her head, then came over to me. "And how are you doing?" she asked.

"What have you done with my car?" I asked her. It sounded like somebody else's voice.

"Don't you worry about that," she said. She put her hand on my forehead. "We'll have you out of here in no time."

"I want my car," I said. I tried to sit up but she held me down. She was stronger than me.

"We just have to make sure you're back to normal," she said.

"*I want my car!*"

STILL

"CNN," THE VOICE on the phone said. "Quick."

"Who is this?" I asked.

"It's your mother."

CNN was broadcasting a live car chase. Helicopter shot from above. A cluster of black-and-white cruisers slowly following a blue pickup through freeway traffic. The sound was off on my set, but I could hear the commentator's distant voice coming from my parents' television. There was a bit of an echo.

"Hello?" my mother asked. "Still there?"

"Where else would I be?"

"It's California," my father said on another extension. "We were there just last year."

"He hijacked the truck," my mother said, "and went on a rampage. He was shooting at people and running stop signs and everything."

"I didn't see any of that," my father said.

"It happened earlier," she said. "The announcer told me while you were in the bathroom." She cleared her throat. "Anyway, I figure he's one of those typical California types. You know the kind I mean."

"A vegetarian?" I asked. "An actor?"

"A druggie," she said, lowering her voice. "And after he hijacked the truck —"

"Wait," I said. "Did he hijack the truck or steal it?"

"What's the difference?" she asked.

"Is there someone in it with him?"

"No. He forced them out at gunpoint."

"That's theft then," I said. "Not hijacking. Hijacking would be if he'd taken them along, if he had hostages."

"Really?"

"I'm pretty sure."

"I had no idea," my mother said.

"Where was I for all this?" my father muttered.

The pickup tried to pass on the shoulder and hit the guardrail, bouncing off and into a white van. Both vehicles stopped for a moment, and the police cruisers slowed. Then the pickup rolled forward again. It drove past one off-ramp after another, hesitating slightly at each one, as if looking for something.

"What I want to know," my mother said, "is where he's going."

There was a long pause, then she added, "So, how are you?"

"Oh, you know," I said. "The same."

"Good, good," she said. "We're fine, too." There were another few seconds of dead air, during which the truck finally took an off-ramp into a run-down neighbourhood, and then she asked, "How's work?"

"All right," I said, even though it had been weeks since I worked.

"That's good," she said. "Because these days ..."

"Yes," I said.

She hummed a little while the truck drove through the parking lot of a boarded-up Kmart. My father belched softly and sighed.

"Crazy from the heat," he said.

"Any new ladies in your life?" my mother suddenly asked.

"No," I said. "There's no one."

"Well, you never know how it'll happen," she said. "Look at your father and me. We met by accident. Isn't that right, hon?"

"Mm-hm."

"I already know the story," I said.

The pickup turned down an alley between warehouses. Zoom out. More cruisers approaching the alley's opposite end. No place to turn around again.

"He called to talk to his cousin," my mother went on, as if she hadn't heard me. "Only she was in the shower. We'd just been sunbathing in the backyard, you see, and we had lotion all over us. I showered later, when I got home. But first I answered the phone, and your father thought I was his cousin. He started talking like he knew me, and he was just so nice and funny that I went along with it. Well, we all had a good laugh about it when he found out, but we'd gotten on so that he asked me out for a date. I said yes, of course, and the next thing I knew, I was walking down the aisle with him. And now here we are. Isn't that right?"

"This is definitely where we are," my father agreed.

Police cruisers blocked both ends of the alley now. The pickup stopped in the middle.

"Things will work out," my mother said.

"I'm not really looking for anything right now," I said.

"Still," she said.

Zoom in. A man in jeans and a white T-shirt jumped out of the pickup. He had a pistol in his hand. He started running for one of the warehouses, and then a little pink cloud puffed from his head. He fell to the ground. Nothing moved but the camera.

"That's gotta hurt," my father said.

"I don't know what things are coming to when this can happen here," my mother sighed.

"It's happening in California," I pointed out.

"Still," she said.

"Well, I should probably go," I said. "Have to get up for work in the morning."

"Wait! Your father hasn't told you his news yet."

"News?" I asked.

Black-clad officers approached the fallen man slowly, guns leveled, like they expected him to rise at any moment.

My father cleared his throat. "You remember my back problems?" he asked. "My crushed verticals?"

"Do you mean your vertebrae?" I asked. Three of them were fused together in his lower back, the result of twenty years driving a truck. He hadn't been able to walk straight in years, let alone work. The doctors had given up on him.

"Yeah," he said, "they're gone."

"What, the vertebrae?"

"No, the problems."

"What do you mean, gone?" I asked. "How could that happen?"

"You know that preacher we like to watch on the television?" he asked.

"Yes," I said slowly.

One of the cops nudged the man with a foot, flipping him over. He stared up at the helicopter, his face a blur from the distance.

"We were watching him the other day," my father said, "when he told everyone he'd been touched by God just before the show started."

"Well, not really God," my mother interrupted. "He said it was an angel whispering in his ear."

"They work for God," my father said. "That's the same thing in my book."

"Your back," I pleaded.

"Right. He said that God told him there'd be a trucker watching that day, one with back problems. He told me to touch the television set. Said he'd heal me if I confessed my sins and believed. So I went and kneeled in front of our television and put my arms around it. And I, ah, I talked about a few different things. But the most important thing is that I was healed. I believed, son."

I had this vision then, of thousands of unemployed truckers across North America — the world, even — kneeling on their shaggy carpets, hugging their television sets, confessing their sins, while their wives looked on and wept.

"And my back problems are gone now," my father finished. "Not so much as an itch left."

"Healed by television," I said.

"Television and God," he said.

"Well." I didn't know what else to say.

"Isn't that something?" my mother asked.

"I really have to go now."

One cop handcuffed the body, and then another cop threw a blanket over it.

"I was there," my mother said. "I saw it all."

IT DOESN'T GET ANY BETTER

I WAS ON MY WAY to Kennedy's wedding, but I couldn't find the church. I tried the Portuguese neighbourhood, the Italian neighbourhood, everywhere. I drove all around the city looking for it. It was called Our Lady of Perpetual Suffering, but all the churches I saw were named after men.

"Why are there so many churches?" I wanted to know. "I mean, who goes to these places?"

Lane, my date, just shook her head and kept brushing hair off herself. She was also my hair stylist, and she was covered in little pieces of hair, each of them a different colour. She was still wearing the same clothes she'd had on when she'd cut my hair: white silk blouse, camouflage pants, black military boots. I'd originally asked Mia to be my date, but I hadn't called her since that incident with the gun.

"Don't you have directions?" Lane asked at one point.

"I had the directions," I explained, "but then I lost them when my apartment was robbed."

"They took the directions?"

"They took everything," I told her. "My whole life."

"What would anybody want with directions to a wedding?"

"What would anybody want with my life?"

I STOPPED AT A 7-ELEVEN to look up the address. Somebody had thrown up in a corner of the phone booth. The churches section of the yellow pages had been ripped out. I looked in the white pages, but there was no listing. It started to rain again while I was in there. When I went back to the car, Lane had a bottle of water and a piece of paper that she passed to me. The directions to the church were written on it.

"Where'd you get this?" I asked.

"I went in to get some water," she said, holding up the bottle. "The guy behind the counter was Hispanic, so I figured he might know where the church was."

"Isn't that racial profiling or something like that?" I asked.

"He gave me the address," she pointed out.

"You've just saved my life," I said. I went to hug her, but she warded me off with the water bottle.

"Remember," she said, "this isn't that kind of date."

I'D ONLY ASKED LANE to be my date that morning, when I was getting my hair cut for the wedding. My appointment was at nine. Lane was the only person working in the salon, although there was a man sleeping on the couch beside the sinks at the back. The phone was ringing the whole time I was in there, but Lane never once looked at it.

"I was at this party last night," she said by way of greeting. "I took these pills and now I can't sleep." She wrapped the apron around me like she was tucking in a child.

"I have a party to go to myself tonight," I said.

"I'm so tired," she went on. "I keep hallucinating, like I'm dreaming even though I'm awake."

"How long do these pills last?" I asked her.

"I don't know," she said. "But if it goes on much longer, I might lose my mind." She laughed as she began cutting my hair, but I wasn't really sure why.

"Well, if you're still up later, maybe you'd like to come to this party," I said.

She stopped cutting and looked at me in the mirror. The man on the couch let out a long sigh and rolled over, but he didn't wake up.

"It's a wedding party," I added. "There'll be lots of other people there."

"You know I'm a dyke, don't you?" she asked.

"That's all right," I said.

"I know it's all right," she said.

"The drinks will be free," I added.

She ruffled my hair with the hand that held the scissors. "As long as we're straight on that," she said.

WE FOUND THE CHURCH between two abandoned warehouses a few blocks away from the 7-Eleven. The building looked like it had once been a garage. The Virgin Mary had been painted over the front door, but someone had spray-painted out the baby Jesus. Now she just held a black circle.

We went inside and found the place empty except for a man in a priest's robe. He was sweeping piles of confetti across the floor, but he paused long enough to look at us. "We're closed for a private event," he said, "but we'll be open again later tonight."

"We're here for the wedding," I said.

"Oh, that." He leaned on the broom and gazed at Lane. "You just missed them," he said.

"But we're not even an hour late," I said, pointing at my watch.

"They were in and out in half an hour," he said. "But they made an awful mess in that time. Someone was even drinking vodka in one of the pews." He nodded at the floor, but I didn't see any bottles anywhere.

"Was it a nice wedding at least?" Lane asked.

"Nice?" The priest looked up at the ceiling of the church. There were spider webs in the rafters. "They called her parents on a cell phone during the ceremony. I had to say all the vows into this phone so they could hear me." He shook his head and went back to sweeping. "I don't know these people," he said. "I've never seen them before, and I doubt I'll ever see them again."

Lane lit a cigarette and looked around the empty room. "I don't suppose they said where they were going?"

"It's all right," I told her. "I know where the reception is."

"You know where it is?" Lane said. "Why didn't we just go there then? We could have skipped this whole church thing."

"If it wasn't for the money," the priest sighed.

"Was there a woman with them?" I asked. "One with a tattoo of Marilyn Monroe here?" I pointed at my stomach, just above my belly button.

"There were women, yes," the priest said, sweeping the confetti towards us, "but I don't know about any tattoos."

"Marilyn Monroe?" Lane asked.

"Let's get out of here," I said to her.

"Everyone always leaves," the priest said, following us with the broom, "but nobody ever comes."

BACK IN THE CAR, Lane laughed and brushed more hair from her clothes. "I can't believe it," she said. "You ask me out on a date, but you're after another woman."

"It's not another woman," I said, "it's my ex-wife."

She looked at me. "Is that supposed to be better?" she asked.

"I heard she'd be here," I said. "I haven't seen her in a year."

"Well, this is certainly going to be an interesting night," Lane said. She took a long drink from the water bottle.

"What do you care, anyway?" I asked. "You're a dyke, remember?"
"Oh, I remember," she said.
"So what does it really matter then?"
"It's the principle of the thing."

THERE WAS A FIGHT going on in the parking lot of the reception hall when we pulled in. There were three or four men involved, I couldn't quite tell, and another three or four standing around, watching. They all stopped what they were doing and looked into the headlights, even the fighters, until we were past them.

"Were those your friends?" Lane asked.

"My friends don't wear rented tuxes," I told her.

I parked beside an SUV with a white dog in the front seat. It was a big dog, the size of a German shepherd but more expensive-looking. It started barking at Lane as soon she got out of the car.

"Hello, doggie," she said in a baby voice and put her hand on the window. The dog bit at the glass, trying to get at her.

"I really don't think you should do that," I said.

"I'd be mad too if I was locked up in this all day," she told the dog. She kicked the side door of the SUV, and its alarm went off. The dog threw itself at the window now, leaving smears of saliva on the glass.

"It's probably thirsty," Lane said. She put the bottle of water up to the open crack at the top of the window and poured the rest of its contents inside. The dog lunged at it, snarling its way through the water. "You see?" Lane said, tossing the empty bottle aside.

We went past the fighting men. There were three of them now, I saw, rolling around on the ground, in and out of puddles formed by the rain. Each of them seemed to be fighting the other two. And the men around them were dirty and wiping blood from their own faces and hands. One of them, who had his arm around the neck of the man beside him, lifted his beer bottle to us as we passed. None of them said anything, though, and the only sound was the grunts of the fighting men. We went inside.

The hall was actually two large rooms separated by a hallway that held the washrooms. There seemed to be a different wedding reception taking place in each room. I looked in the room to the right but didn't recognize anyone there. The bride was dancing in the middle of the room to an old Whitney Houston song. She looked as if her nose had been broken a number of times. I wasn't sure, but I thought the man she was dancing with might have been her father. She also looked as if she wouldn't be able to stand up without his help. Everyone else was sitting at their tables, watching them dance.

"Are these your friends?" Lane asked.

"Do these look like my friends?" I asked.

"I really wouldn't know," she said.

"These don't look like anybody's friends," I said.

We went into the other room. All the tables had been pulled to the walls here, and everyone was dancing in the empty space in the middle of the room. I didn't recognize the music, and I also didn't recognize most of the people here. I looked around for Kennedy and spotted him by the gift table, taking photos of the crowd with a digital camera.

"This way," I told Lane.

"I think I'm going to get a drink," she said. She pushed her way through the crowd, to the bar on the other side of the room.

Kennedy was staring at a picture of himself in the camera when I got to him. "We just missed you at the church," I told him.

He looked up from the camera and grinned when he saw me. "Hey, I thought maybe you weren't going to make it," he said.

"I don't think I know anyone here," I said.

"These things are like high school reunions," he said, nodding.

"Where is she?" I asked, glancing around the room.

He pointed to a woman on the dance floor. She was in the middle of the crowd but she was dancing alone, as everyone kept a few feet away from her. Her eyes were closed. She was wearing a white bridal gown. I actually took a step toward her before I realized she didn't look anything like Rachel.

"Who's that?" I asked.

"That's my wife," Kennedy said.

The more I stared at her, the more familiar she looked. Then I remembered her. She was one of the women that Kennedy had danced with that night I'd gone over to his place and wound up with Mia. He didn't even know her then, and now here he was, marrying her.

"Where's my wife?" I asked.

"What are you talking about?" Kennedy asked, looking at me.

"You told me Rachel would be here," I said.

"I don't know where Rachel is," he said, shaking his head.

"You said she'd be here when you invited me to the wedding," I said. "You said you'd found her."

"I said I'd found some *photographs* of Rachel," Kennedy said. "I said I'd bring them to the wedding." He handed the camera to me. "They're in here, somewhere near the beginning."

I looked down at the camera in my hand. It was warm from him holding it, and slick with sweat. "So she's not here?" I asked.

"She's never been here," he said and moved off into the crowd.

I started to go through the pictures in the camera, looking for Rachel, but just then Lane appeared at my side, a gin and tonic in each hand. "You have to pay for the drinks here," she said.

"All right," I said.

"You said they'd be free," she went on.

"I'll get them," I told her.

"I've already paid for these ones," she said, "but you're getting the rest." She took a sip of one of the drinks, then she saw Kennedy's wife. She watched her for a moment and then smiled. "I think I'm going to dance now," she said.

I went around the edge of the room, looking for a quiet place where I could sit down and look at the pictures in the camera. But there were people everywhere, standing or sitting in groups, talking and laughing and watching me pass. I went out into the hall, just as Kennedy was coming out of the restroom.

"Hey, let me see that for a moment," he said, taking the camera from me. He went up to the door of the other room and started taking photos.

"What are you doing?" I asked him. "That's not your party."

"Don't you think I know that?" he said. He took a photo of the other bride as she ran past him and outside. She was gagging and covering her mouth with one hand, while dragging one of the bridesmaids behind her with the other. "This is going to make a great album," Kennedy said.

"Be careful with that," I told him. "I haven't looked at all the pictures yet."

He didn't answer me, though, because just then one of the fighting men from outside came in and saw him standing there with the camera. "What the hell do you think you're doing?" this man asked.

Kennedy didn't answer him, just grinned and took his picture.

"You goddamn perverts," the other man said. He lunged forward, but Kennedy stepped behind me, so the man hit me instead, punching me in the face. I fell backward, into Kennedy, who shoved me forward again, back at the other man. He caught me, holding me in his arms for what seemed like moments, and then dropped me to the wood-tiled floor. Down here, everything smelled like lemons.

When I managed to lift my head again, I saw Kennedy wrestling with the other man. The camera had fallen to the floor, and the other man was stomping on it while holding Kennedy in a headlock. Little pieces of the camera were flying everywhere.

I screamed and grabbed hold of the man's foot. He was wearing one of those shiny dress shoes, the kind you can only get with rented tuxes. He screamed back at me and tried to kick me with his other foot but lost his balance instead. He fell to the floor, taking Kennedy with him, and I heard rather than saw his head bounce off the floor. I got on my knees and grabbed the camera, looked at the picture screen. It was black, a crack running straight down the middle of it. I hit every button I could see on the camera. The screen stayed black.

"Jesus," Kennedy said behind me, "I think you killed him."

I turned around and looked at the other man. He was spasming on the floor, limbs jerking back and forth, his eyes rolled back so only the whites were showing.

"Me?" I said. "You were the one who started this." I could barely breathe. I thought I was going to faint.

"But you were the one who kicked his ass," Kennedy said. He pulled me to my feet and put his arms around me. "This is the best wedding I've been to yet," he said and kissed me.

It wasn't what I really wanted, but it was something.

LATER, WHEN THE other groom — I knew he was the other groom because he was the only person wearing a white jacket — came in and started fighting with Kennedy, I went back into Kennedy's reception room to get Lane. She was dancing with Kennedy's wife, and when I went up to them and told her I was leaving, she just waved me away. I went back into the hall again. Kennedy and the other groom were rolling around on the floor and over the guy having the seizure, biting and clawing at each other and laughing. I went back out into the rain.

Outside, the other bride was sitting in the middle of the parking lot. Somehow, the white dog from the SUV had gotten loose and it was attacking her, trying to get underneath her wedding gown to bite at her ankles. She'd kick it away, and then it would come back again, lunging underneath the gown. The white silk was torn all along the bottom of the dress now and stained from sitting on the wet ground. The woman was crying when I walked past her. "I just want to go home," she kept saying to the dog. It barked at her and didn't pay any attention to me at all.

I stopped and watched this for a moment, then said, "I'll give you a ride." I helped her to her feet. She'd lost one of her shoes somewhere, so she took my arm as I led her to the car. The dog followed, growling and biting at her heels.

There was a couple making out in the front seat of the SUV. I wasn't sure if they were the owners or not, because the car alarm was still going off. I unlocked the passenger door of my car, and the woman got in. The dog got up on its hind legs and looked in at her as soon as I closed the door. Its tail was wagging furiously.

"Where are you staying?" I asked her when I got in on the driver's side.

"The Holiday Inn," she said. She'd stopped crying now, but she made no move to wipe the mascara from her face. There was still a bit of vomit on her chin. She looked like a raccoon.

"Is that where your husband's staying?" I asked.

"Of course that's where he's staying," she said. "Where else would he go?"

"I just want to make sure he'll know where to find you," I told her.

On the way out of the parking lot, the headlights caught a fox in the shrubs. It looked like it had a kitten in its mouth, but I wasn't certain because it ran off.

"Is this your first wedding?" I asked the woman.

"This is my only wedding," she said. Then, "Do you have any cigarettes?"

"I don't smoke," I said. "But I'm sure you can get some from one of the hotel's vending machines."

"I don't have any money," she said.

"It's your wedding night," I said. "Think of all the money you just made."

"No, what I mean is that this dress doesn't have any pockets."

"On our wedding night," I went on, "we piled all the money we got on the bed and made love in it. We didn't even count it until we were done. Nearly six thousand dollars. We left a hundred-dollar tip for the maid. For luck, my wife said."

"Where's your wife now?" she asked me.

"She's dead," I told her. It was true. I knew now I was never going to see Rachel again.

"Oh, I'm sorry," the woman said.

I shook my head. "I've never had that much money since," I said.

She didn't say anything for a moment, just looked out the side window. I could see strands of the dog's saliva still on the window, trapped in her reflection. "This is it then," she sighed. "The best night of my life."

"It doesn't get any better," I agreed.

THERE'S NOTHING WRONG WITH ME

I WAS WORKING as an actor. I got the job through a number Eden gave me after they let him out of jail. When I called the number, the woman who answered told me to come in to the office so she could see what I looked like. She didn't want to know anything else about me.

"Should I bring a resumé?" I asked.

"If you like," she said, "but it's not really necessary."

"What about references?" I asked. "I'm sure I could find somebody to give me a good reference."

"It's not really that kind of job," she said.

"But don't you need to know about my work experience and all that?"

"All I need to know is that you look normal."

The office was a studio in an east-end warehouse. There were Asian men working behind computers in the room next to it. They stared at me as I walked past but they never stopped typing. A fan blew the smell of sweat out into the hallway.

The walls of the office I went into were lined with old movie posters and black-and-white photographs of people I didn't recognize. Half the office was taken up with sealed packing boxes. The woman I'd talked to on the phone sat behind the desk that was in the other half of the room. She was dressed in shorts and a black T-shirt, and she was playing solitaire on her computer when I walked in.

She just looked at me for a moment after I introduced myself, then nodded to herself. "I guess you look all right," she said, "but I need to ask you a few questions." She motioned for me to sit in one of the two chairs, then pulled a form out of her desk. There was a coffeemaker with a full pot of coffee sitting on the windowsills, but she didn't offer me anything to drink.

"Do you have a car?" she asked.

"Yes."

"Have you ever threatened a co-worker with violence or stolen from your employer?"

"That's one question?"

She tapped her pen on the table but didn't say anything.

"No," I said.

"Bondable?"

"What does all this have to do with acting?" I asked.

"I should tell you now," she said, gazing out the window, "that this job will not lead to any big breaks in the movie industry."

"Bondable," I said.

"Have you ever tried to associate with any actors against their will or followed them without their knowledge?"

"Not really," I said.

"Not really," she repeated, looking back at me again. "Now what does that mean?"

"No," I said.

She made a few more notes, which I couldn't see because she

shielded them with her hand, then put the form back in the desk.

"So, do you have a job for me?" I asked her.

"I have the perfect job for you," she said.

THE AGENCY GOT ME a television commercial job. I was paid seventy dollars and a free breakfast for an hour's work. There were fifty of us, all from different agencies around the city. We were playing the parts of business people on our way to work. The shoot took place in front of the stock exchange downtown. The street was blocked off at either end with yellow tape. We walked along the sidewalk in front of the cameras in small groups, carrying briefcases and bags the costumes woman had given us. I was wearing the same suit that I'd worn the day I married Rachel.

The assistant director briefed us at the beginning of the shoot. He was chewing gum rapidly and his hands shook the whole time he talked to us. "Look like you have somewhere important to go," he said. "But don't overact — you're just the background for the shot." It was the only direction anyone ever gave us. The only other people who spoke to us were the production assistants, two women in baseball caps and sunglasses who stood at either side of the set and told us when to walk in front of the cameras. They kept coffee cups to their lips the whole time, breathing in the steam even when they weren't drinking. It was five in the morning. The buildings all around us were lit up even though no one was in them yet.

I watched the shooting from the side of the set while waiting my turn to walk in front of the cameras. The stars, two men in nicer suits than anyone else's, stood talking at the edge of the sidewalk while the extras walked at least five feet behind them.

"They have to keep them on a different plane," one of the other extras, a black man with a French accent, told me. "Or the audience won't know who's important."

One of the stars was Mercedes's boyfriend, the man that I'd whipped in The Code that day. I was afraid that he would see me and have me kicked off the set. But he looked right at me during a break in the filming and he didn't even blink.

There was garbage everywhere on the streets that morning. When it was my turn to walk in front of the camera, the wind carried a stray piece of newspaper into my leg. I tried to shake it off, but it wrapped around my leg. There was a photograph of a group of firemen standing around a burning tanker truck on the outside page. I bent down to pull it off, but the man with the French accent bumped into me from behind. "Keep going," he hissed. I kept walking until I was at the edge of the set. The newspaper remained on my leg the whole time.

The real business people began showing up a few hours after we began shooting. They stood behind the tape at the edges of the set, checking their watches and waiting for us to finish. Those of us who'd already been in the shoot stood around the food tables, eating muffins and drinking lukewarm coffees. While I watched, a pair of men in tan overcoats and black briefcases stepped around the tape and walked through the set the same way we had, while the cameras were rolling, and went into the building. No one seemed to notice.

They wrapped the shoot a few minutes after that. The production assistants took down the tape while the camera crews cleared the street. Suddenly there were young men in shorts and baseball caps everywhere, coiling cables or moving lights. The costumes woman collected all the briefcases from the extras. Within moments you couldn't tell there had been a film shoot there at all, except for the trailers and the extras still standing around in a group. I had no idea where the stars had gone.

I found myself beside the man with the French accent again. "Well, now what?" I asked.

"Now we wait for the cheque," he said. "If it takes any longer than a week, call your agent. These guys may not be in business a month from now."

"You do a lot of this kind of thing?" I asked.

"This is *all* I do," he said.

"So television commercials are your job?"

"Blending in is my job," he said.

Most of the other extras went down the street to catch the bus, but I went over to where one of the cameramen was pouring himself a cup of coffee. "How did I look?" I asked him.

He squinted at me and said, "Who are you?"

"I'm one of the extras," I said. "I had the newspaper on my leg."

"Oh, right." He took a pill from his pocket and ground it up in his hand, dropped the powder into his coffee.

"I'm just wondering how everything worked out," I said. "Did I look real?"

"Oh yeah," he said, stirring the powder under. "Better than real."

THE AGENCY GOT ME all kinds of shoots. Once, I was hired to be an audience member for a new talk show. We shot it in the middle of the night, in a downtown studio. I sat between a woman doing a crossword puzzle and a man who looked under his seat when he sat down. "Sometimes the day show puts prizes there and people forget to take them," he explained to me. "Or sometimes people just forgot what they brought."

"The day show?" I said.

"That's the show the set belongs to," he said, nodding at the stage. There was nothing up there but a beige backdrop and four chairs that had been taken from the back row of the audience. "It's been on for years."

"But they changed the chairs," the woman on my other side said. "The day show has those upholstered ones."

"Oh yeah," the man said. "They wouldn't want to waste those on this operation."

"The day show *is* those chairs," the woman added.

The host came out of the back just then and started talking to the one cameraman. He still wore the cloth to protect his suit from the makeup. His skin looked orange.

"How many times have you worked for this show?" I asked the man beside me.

"This is the first time," he said. "It's the pilot."

"But you've worked here before," I said.

"There's one of these pilots every week," he said.

"And how many of them make it to air?" I asked.

"I haven't seen any yet," he said. "But all it takes is one."

A man wearing a headset and carrying a plastic bag walked over and said to me, "You have to take that shirt off."

I looked down at my shirt. It was a plain black T-shirt. "But it's all I have," I said.

"Too many T-shirts in the crowd," he said. "Everyone looks unemployed. We need some professional-type people." He reached into the bag and took out a white button-down, tossed it at me. "Just remember to give that back when the shoot's over."

I took off my T-shirt and dropped it under my chair, put on the button-down. My skin started itching right away. I couldn't stop thinking of lice and crabs.

The host gave us a speech before they started the show. He was still wearing his makeup cloth. "Remember," he said, "we're the new kind of talk show. We don't want people sitting on their chairs clapping when the applause sign comes on and then stopping when it goes off."

"Do they even have the budget for an applause sign?" the woman beside me asked.

"We want people throwing their chairs," the host went on. "We want confrontation. Conflict. Drama. Spectacle. Don't be afraid to shout things out or do something spontaneous. If you're exciting enough, we may even get picked up."

"He gave the exact same speech with the last pilot," the man beside me muttered.

The host walked to the center of the stage and nodded at the camera. The man who'd made me change shirts ran up and yanked off the host's makeup cloth, then went to the edge of the stage and held up a sign that had Quiet hand-painted on it.

"Welcome to The Zone," the host said to the camera, "your new guide to the afternoon."

The woman beside me rolled her eyes and looked at the ceiling. The man on my other side looked under my chair and picked up a dime off the floor.

"You'll like today's show," the host said. "It's about people who are afraid of the end of the world."

The man with the Quiet sign yelled "Cut!" and the host sat on one of the chairs while the cameraman moved the camera into a new position.

"This is a sorry fucking operation," the man beside me sighed.

"Isn't everyone afraid of the end of the world?" the woman on my other side asked.

The first guest was a man in a military uniform. The host told the camera that he was a colonel in the army.

"Ex-colonel," the other man said. "They kicked me out on account of me revealing all their dirty little secrets."

"What secrets are those?" the host asked.

The ex-colonel leaned forward and glanced between the host and the camera. "They're already poisoning us slowly," he said in a stage whisper.

"Who's poisoning us?" the host asked.

"The government," the ex-colonel said. "They're putting chemicals and nuclear waste in the water. Next it'll be a nuclear device in one of our cities. Maybe not a full-scale one, but a dirty nuke at least."

"Why would they do that?" the host asked.

"So they can increase our taxes," the ex-colonel said. "On account of the threat and all."

"What exactly does all this have to do with the end of the world?" the host asked.

The ex-colonel leaned back in his chair. "Where there's one nuke, there's more," he said. "You can make them with intel from the Internet now. All it takes is one to start, and pretty soon everyone's blowing one off in the back of a rental truck."

"I don't know," the host said, shaking his head. "Let's see what the audience thinks." He looked out at us, and for a moment no one said anything. The ex-colonel cleared his throat several times.

I raised my hand. The host quickly pointed at me. "You have something to say," he said. The man and woman beside me turned and stared.

"I think you've been watching too much television," I told the ex-colonel.

"Yes!" the host said, nodding. The man who'd been holding the Quiet sign now held up a sign that had Applause painted on it, and audience members here and there clapped.

"It's all true," the ex-colonel said.

"I don't think so," I said.

"Haven't you been watching the news?" the ex-colonel asked.

"In fact," I went on, "I think I saw that very movie last week." The man with the sign raised it over his head and more people applauded.

The ex-colonel stood up, knocking his chair over as he did so. "All right," he said, "pretend like nothing's happening." He walked off the stage and into the back area. He paused just before going around the backdrop. "But don't say I didn't warn you when you're nothing but a shadow burned into the side of a building."

"I saw that show too," I said.

"What is wrong with you?" the man beside me asked when the ex-colonel was gone and the crew were getting ready for the next segment.

"I know, I know," I said. "That guy has probably been trained how to kill me a thousand different ways."

"I think I went to theatre school with him," the woman on my other side said.

The second segment of the show was a family. A balding husband in a navy blazer, a daughter with braces, a mother with black hair and red-framed glasses. This was Iris, although I didn't know her name at the time. The host asked them what they were afraid of.

"Asteroids," the husband said. "It's only a matter of time before a planet-killer hits us."

"We've seen that movie too," the host said, looking at the audience and rolling his eyes.

"Tell that to the dinosaurs," the husband said.

"What about you, darling?" the host asked the daughter. "What are you afraid of?"

"Nuclear meltdown," the girl said. "Radioactive fallout that kills all the livestock and causes cancer for hundreds of miles away from the epicenter. Firestorms. Nuclear winter. Entire cities abandoned. Outbreaks of disease. Foot and mouth. Tuberculosis. AIDS."

The host just looked at her.

"Like that Chernobyl show," the girl added.

"We've been letting her watch A&E," the husband said, nodding and smiling.

"And what about you?" the host asked, turning to Iris. "What are you afraid of?"

"God," Iris said.

"God," the host repeated. He looked at the camera and smiled, but it didn't reach his eyes.

"God is the atom," Iris said. "Remember, when Oppenheimer saw the atomic bomb explode at Los Alamos, he said, 'Lo, I am become God, destroyer of worlds.'"

"Who's this Oppenheimer?" the host asked, frowning. "Is he a terrorist or something?"

"God is our destroyer," Iris went on, "and only God can save us from himself." She dropped off her chair, to her knees. "Let us pray."

The host didn't know what to say. He looked to us for help.

Iris dragged her husband and daughter down to the floor with her. The little girl actually started to cry. "Who will join us?" Iris asked. She looked out over the audience, and our eyes met. She stared at me for a few seconds, and then I was up out of my chair and pushing past the woman beside me and running up to kneel on the stage too. The host's jaw actually dropped as I went past him.

Iris took my hand and smiled at me. Then she looked straight into the camera. "Heavenly father, destroyer of worlds," she began.

How could I not fall in love with her?

AS IT TURNED OUT, Iris worked for the same agency as me. Once, it got us work together in a commercial. This one was in a burned-out warehouse across the city. The shoot took place in the front lobby. It was just one scene: Iris and I had to walk hand in hand across the lobby, which the crew had cleaned and filled with fake potted plants. We were in the background of the shot.

"What's in the foreground?" I asked the woman in charge as she directed the cameramen where to set up their equipment.

"I don't know," she said. "They're going to add it in later with computers."

"What's the product?" I asked.

She shook her head. "I don't know that either."

"But people will still be able to see us, right?" I asked.

"Oh yeah," she said, "you'll be stars."

Iris had a son who came to the shoot with her. This was her real son — the family from the talk show worked for our agency too. This boy was in a wheelchair, and when I looked close I could tell there was something not quite right about him. He had the body of a boy, but his skin was all wrinkled and his hair was starting to fall out, like he was an old man. Iris parked his wheelchair to the side of one of the cameras, where he could watch us work. He had a camera of his own — a digital one — and he filmed the crew setting up with it.

I asked Iris what was wrong with him while she was doing her stretching exercises.

"He's got that aging disease," she said, not looking up at me.

"Is it fatal?" I asked.

"Aging usually is," she said.

"What's his name?" I asked.

"Walker," Iris said.

"Isn't that a little ironic?" I asked.

"I don't know what you mean," she said, doing the splits and touching her head to the floor.

I wandered around the place while we were waiting. The rest of the warehouse was divided into large rooms, each holding different appliances. One room was full of televisions stacked on skids that had been put down in loose, winding rows. Another room was full of fridges and microwaves, their white exteriors scorched by the fire that had closed down the place. Another room was computers piled loosely on the floor. For some reason, the monitor on each one had been smashed. Water dripped from the ceiling in each of the rooms, and I could still smell smoke.

Back in the lobby, I asked the woman in charge what kind of warehouse this was.

"I don't know," she said, "I think it was one of those places they stored things that nobody wants any more."

"Who wouldn't want all of this?" I wondered.

"I mean, I think it's stuff that's not in fashion any more," she said. "You know, things that got old before people were done with them."

"Oh, I know all about that," I said, but she didn't answer because the cameramen were yelling that they were ready for the shot. Iris and I took our places.

We walked across the room, hand in hand. Iris's palm was moist in mine, and I could feel her heartbeat when our wrists touched. When we were done, I asked the woman in charge how it looked.

"You're supposed to be in love," she said, shaking her head.

"Oh, we are," I said. "See?" I was still holding Iris's hand.

"Then try to show it more."

"How would we do that?" Iris asked.

"A look," the other woman said. "A smile. Something."

"How about a kiss?" I suggested.

"Let's not get carried away here," Iris said.

We went over to where Walker sat in his wheelchair. He'd filmed all this but he put the camera down when we approached.

"Did you get it?" Iris asked.

Walker nodded but didn't say anything.

"What are you filming this for?" I asked.

"It's for the archives," Iris said.

"I see," I said, although I didn't. I reached out and ruffled Walker's hair, and when I brought my hand away, there were individual strands of hair clinging to it.

"Please don't do that," Iris told me. "He needs all he's got."

When they were ready with the cameras once more, Iris and I went and did the shot again. This time I looked over at her and smiled as we walked. She smiled back. I squeezed her hand. She squeezed mine back. It was like we were actually a couple.

"That was better," the woman in charge said when we had crossed the lobby. "One more time, just in case."

Iris went to talk to Walker again, but he was gone now. His wheelchair was still there, but it was empty except for the camera on the seat. "Walker?" she called, looking around. "Where are you?"

"You mean he can actually walk?" I asked.

"Of course he can walk," she said, pausing to look at me. "What did you think?"

"So the wheelchair is just for show?" I asked.

"Walker!" she cried, turning in a circle.

The woman in charge came over. "What's the problem?" she asked.

"Our son is missing," I told her.

"We have to find him," Iris said. "I don't know where I'd be without him."

"We'll organize a search party," I said to the woman in charge. "We'll divide up into teams and mark things off on grids and stuff."

"You go ahead," she said. "We're going to set up for the shot again. Try to find him before we're ready."

Iris and I went into the room with all the refrigerators and microwaves. "Walker!" she cried again. She opened a freezer and looked inside, like he was hiding in there.

"Maybe he was mad at us," I said, "on account of the shoot and all."

"What are you talking about?" she asked, looking at me.

"I saw this show once," I said, "where these kids were upset because their parents had started dating after the divorce or death or whatever it was that had taken place. Maybe Walker's upset because of this couple thing we're doing here."

"Maybe we should split up to look for him," Iris said. "I'll take that room with all the computers."

"Where do you want me to look?" I asked.

"Anywhere but there," she said.

"All right," I said to myself after she was gone, looking around the empty room. "Where would I go if I were lost?"

I found Walker in the room with all the dead televisions. I heard him before I saw him. He was making this mewling noise.

I followed it around the maze of televisions. I ran into several dead ends and had to backtrack before I finally found him. He was sitting on the floor in front of a big-screen television with a broken screen. He was crying, but he didn't stop when he saw me.

"There you are," I said. "We've been worried sick about you." I put out my arms, but he just looked at the broken television and kept on crying. I picked him up and carried him back to the lobby.

They were set up for the shot again by the time I made it back there, but now everyone was on a coffee break.

"It's about time," the woman in charge said as I put Walker back in his chair. "I was beginning to worry."

"So was I," I said.

"Another hour and we have to pay the crew overtime," she said.

We waited for Iris to come back, but she didn't. "Maybe she's lost too," I said. "Maybe I'll have to rescue her as well."

The woman in charge looked at her watch. "Maybe we should just go with what we've got."

Walker wouldn't stop crying, so I patted him on the head. "You're okay," I said. "There's nothing wrong with you." But still he kept on.

I took the camera from him and rewound it until I found a shot of Iris and me walking across the lobby together. I paused it and held the camera out to Walker. "Look," I said, "there's your mom."

He stopped crying and took the camera. He put it in his lap and stared down at the image.

"You see?" I said. "Everything's all right."

AND ONCE THE AGENCY got Iris and me work as mannequins at the downtown mall. One of the department stores was having a promotion and wanted live people modeling clothes in a display window. We changed into their clothes, and the man in charge, Tiff, walked us to the display. "I have to lock the door when you're inside," he said, "on account of store regulations and all, but I'll let you out every hour for a washroom break."

"What do you want us to do?" I asked once we were inside the display case.

"Just act natural," Tiff said.

"This isn't exactly a natural setting," I told him.

"What I mean is that I don't want you to act like mannequins," he said. "I want you to act like people."

"I can do that," I said.

"I hope so," he said, "because that's why we hired you."

"I've been acting like a person all my life."

The display window was where the store met the rest of the mall. The inside of it was set up like a living room and kitchen. There was a couch, a television, chairs, lamps, a stove and refrigerator, the whole works. It was all from the store. It was the kind of place I dreamed about living in.

Iris and I sat on the couch and watched a DVD on the television. It was one of those expensive DVD players, the kind that held six discs, so we could have sat there and watched movies for the entire shift, but after a half hour or so, Tiff opened the door to the case and told us we had to be more dynamic.

"I don't know what you mean," I said.

"Move around," he said. "Use *all* the products."

I got up and went over to the fridge. It was plugged in and full of bottles of water. I opened one and drank from it. Outside, in the mall, people stopped to look at us. I waved at them. Tiff pounded on the glass wall of the display and shook his head.

Iris went over to the exercise bike in the corner and started cycling. She was still watching the movie. I took a water bottle over to her.

"What are you doing?" she asked, looking at it.

"I'm bringing you water," I said.

"Why?" she asked, looking at me now.

"I'm trying to pretend like we're a couple," I said. "On account of the display and all." I leaned in and kissed her on the cheek.

She shook her head but took the water. "I need to find another job," she said.

"This is the best job I've ever had," I said.

IRIS AND I WORKED as mannequins for a couple of weeks. When we were on break, I liked to stand out in the hallway, looking in at the display case. Sometimes I even polished the window with paper towel and glass cleaner I got from one of the women who worked the perfume counters.

After a few days, Iris started bringing Walker to work. She parked his wheelchair in front of the display case, where he could watch us. He filmed us all day long with his digital camera.

On one of our breaks, I tried talking to him. Iris was off in the washroom or buying food or something, so it was just the two of us.

"How's it going, son?" I asked him.

He turned the camera on me but didn't say anything. The one eye I could see was closed so he could look through the camera's viewfinder.

"Maybe someday we can take you in there with us," I said, indicating the display. "Would you like that?"

He still didn't say anything, just kept on filming.

"All right then," I said and looked back at the case. Out of the corner of my eye, I saw him turn the camera back on it too.

When Iris came back, she asked us what we had been doing.

"We were bonding," I said, and Walker laughed.

THE MANNEQUIN JOB ENDED for us when I lit the display case on fire. I'd brought in some soup and I was heating it in a pot on the stove when I smelled something burning. I lifted the pot and looked underneath but there was nothing on the element.

"Now what have you done?" Iris asked, coming over from where she'd been doing jumping jacks in the middle of the living room.

"I haven't done anything," I said. But when I turned off the stove, the smell grew even stronger. Then Walker rolled his wheelchair over until he was directly on the other side of the glass from us, and he pointed behind the stove. I looked back there. The curtains that were framing the fake window over the stove hung down where all the electrical outlets for the display were, and the bottom part of them was on fire.

"How did you manage that?" Iris asked.

"I didn't do it," I said. "It must be some sort of wiring thing."

"Well, we should put it out," Iris said.

I threw the soup on the curtains, but it only put out some of the fire. The case was beginning to grow hazy with smoke now, and the people who had been watching Iris do jumping jacks started to back away.

"Now what?" I said.

"Now I think we should leave," Iris said.

But when we went to the door, it was locked. "Tiff!" I shouted, banging on the door, but he was nowhere in sight. The only people from the store I could see were the women from the perfume counter, and they just stayed by their counter and stared at us. I ran to the phone on our end table, picked it up, and dialed 911 before I realized there was no dial tone.

Iris was at the other end of the display case, shouting to Walker through the glass. "Don't let anyone take the camera away from you if we die," she said. "You'll need that film for the lawsuit." He nodded and kept filming.

Now the curtains were totally on fire, and the flames had spread to other things. The fake window frame was burning, as was the edge of the carpet. And there was a thick layer of smoke at the top of the case.

"Why isn't there a fire extinguisher in here?" I asked. "Every home should have a fire extinguisher."

Iris ran to my side. "Have you got any ideas how to get us out of this mess?" she said.

"We should lie down," I said. "In the movies, people always lie down to get away from the smoke."

"We don't need to get away from the smoke," she said, "we need to get away from *here*. We need to break the glass."

"I don't know," I said, looking at the large windows. The display case was completely ringed by people watching us now. "What if they charge us for that?"

"Oh my God," Iris said and ran to one of the walls. "Help!" she screamed, pounding on the wall and waving at the crowd. "Someone help me!"

I saw then that it was up to me. I went over to the television and picked it up. It was a big-screen model, and I could barely lift it. I staggered over to the wall that Iris was pounding on and threw it at the glass.

The wall shattered as the television went through it, and large pieces of glass fell out into the mall. Some people in the crowd screamed and ran away, but others applauded. Iris pushed past me and jumped to the floor, then ran to Walker. I followed her but only made it about halfway before I collapsed to the floor. Now that I was in the fresh air of the mall, I could barely breathe — all I could do was cough.

I looked back at the display case in time to see Tiff rush into it with a fire extinguisher. Everything was burning now — the rug, the couch, even the fake flowers on the kitchen table. Tiff sprayed wildly with the fire extinguisher for a moment, but it ran out of foam before he'd even put out the couch. Then his pants caught on fire. He ran out of the display case, burning and screaming, in the direction of the women at the perfume counter, who scattered at his approach.

But that was all I saw, because then I was rolling over and throwing up on the floor. After I was done throwing up, I passed out.

At least, I think I passed out, because the next thing I knew, I was on my back and staring at the sign of the Starbucks across the hall, while people from the crowd kneeled all around me. I opened my mouth to speak but couldn't get any words out.

Iris was at my side, and she rested her hand on my forehead. "You're going to be all right," she said. "I think someone's called an ambulance."

I looked around at everyone staring down at me. All those people concerned about me — I almost couldn't believe it.

My whole body started to shake, and Iris moved her hand from my forehead to my chest, pressing me down to the mall floor. "You're going to be all right," she said again, but I couldn't stop shaking.

Walker rolled up on the other side of me. For a moment our eyes met, even as I continued shaking. Then he held out the camera so I could see the image there. It was of the time that I'd kissed Iris in the display case, before the fire.

"You're okay," he said. "There's nothing wrong with you."

"That's right," Iris said. "There's nothing wrong with you."

I couldn't stop shaking but I nodded.

"Say it," Iris said.

I couldn't look away from that picture.

"Say it," Iris said again.

"There's nothing wrong with me," I managed.

ACKNOWLEDGEMENTS

Excerpts from *Please* have appeared in the following: *Blood & Aphorisms, Canadian Fiction, The I.V. Lounge Reader, Queen Street Quarterly, Taddle Creek.*

Special thanks to: Denise Bedard, Jonathan Bennett, Michelle Berry, Marlene Darbyshire, Phillip Darbyshire, Ralf Darbyshire, Patrick Deane, Stan Dragland, Joy Gugeler, Wendy Morgan, Elaine O'Connor, Amanda Undseth, Paul Vermeersch, WORDS.

Thanks also to the K.M. Hunter Foundation, the Ontario Arts Council, and the Toronto Arts Council for financial support.

PETER DARBYSHIRE has published fiction and articles in journals and papers across North America. He lives in Toronto, where he works as a freelance reviewer and writer.

PHOTO: JENNIFER ROWSOM RHODES

Please is typeset in FF Scala, designed by Martin Majoor in 1988 for the Vredenburg Music Centre in Utrecht, Netherlands. With its complementary sans serif FF Scala Sans, FF Scala is the typeface that appears in the second largest news-paper in Holland (*Algemeen Dagblad*). Scala appears fine, light and elegant, yet a close look reveals an even stroke weight, square serifs and simple curves. The letterforms reflect both the fine French and sturdy Dutch type traditions.

Polestar and Raincoast Books are committed to protecting the environment and to the responsible use of natural resources. We are acting on this commitment by working with suppliers and printers to phase out our use of paper produced from ancient forests. This book is one step towards that goal. It is printed on Eco Book, a 100% ancient-forest-free paper (100% post-consumer recycled), processed chlorine- and acid-free, and supplied by New Leaf Paper. It is printed with vegetable-based inks by Friesens in Altona, Manitoba.